ENEMY WOLF

HOWLING DEATH MC
BOOK TWO

SOPHIE ASH

CONTENT WARNING

This book contains the following:

- Explicit sex scenes
- Scarring/marking
- Violent fight scenes
- Mentions of abusive partners (not the main characters)
- Mentions of abusive parental figures
- Mating bites/marks

CHAPTER 1
SHILOH

By the fucking moon, this could not be happening.

Someone was *not* breaking into my bar right now.

But I could hear the footfalls from where I was doing inventory in the back storage room, and my disbelief was not lining up with reality.

The floorboards creaked under the weight of the intruder and I froze, holding my breath to listen. This person was large, most likely a man. They moved slowly across the room, as if taking care where they stepped. From back here, I couldn't tell if they were going for the cash drawer or somewhere else. For all I knew, it was some rogue vampire who'd come to vandalize my place just because I was near the border of Sanguine, the vampire territory.

I frowned at that thought. Derric, the Howling Death alpha, said the vampires wouldn't bother us anymore. But who else could it be? My bar, Stout & Spirit, was the most popular watering hole in Vargmore, the werewolf territory, despite my not being a werewolf. I knew just about everyone who came through—which was the entirety of Vargmore, pretty much.

I couldn't think of a single citizen who would break into my place of business, aside from some naughty children with no malicious intent. But whoever was on the other side of that door was no child, not even a gangly teenager.

So it could only be a longtime enemy of the werewolves, either the vampires or the dragon shifters.

As I went for my phone, the footfalls stopped just outside the storage room door, and I froze again. I thought I heard sniffing, and then a deep male voice muttering to himself on the other side before continuing on.

Scenting the air was a very werewolf thing to do, which again, was odd. My mind flicked through the hundreds of faces I knew, all wolves I was at least somewhat acquainted with. None of them seemed like the type to break in, so what the fuck?

I scrolled through my phone, trying not to breathe too loudly while also calming my racing heart. My thumb hovered over Sawyer's number, Howling Death's enforcer.

And my ex-boyfriend, of sorts.

I chewed my lip, for some reason hesitant to call him up. He was newly mated, for one, and at this hour, probably spending some quality time with Riley. And despite him ending things between us abruptly and then falling head over heels for her soon after, I actually liked his mate and didn't want to impose on them.

Yeah, I was *such* a good friend. As I so often heard.

I also considered the possibility that I didn't need him to come to my rescue. I may not have been a werewolf, but I was something even, dare I say, better.

A witch.

I may not have had teeth and claws, but I certainly had

other tricks up my sleeve. And damn it, this was *my* bar. I didn't need to cry to the wolves for help with every little thing.

Determined, I went for the baseball bat stashed in the corner behind the door. A bar patron had brought it in months ago, saying he'd gone to a game in the human world and gotten it from a player as a souvenir. We didn't have baseball in Shyftworld, though I'd seen it on some human TV channels. I'd taken it away from the patron for swinging the bat a little too enthusiastically in the dining area. He'd been drunk enough to leave without it and hadn't come back for it since.

"Thank you, Sacramento Rivercats," I muttered, hovering my left hand over the thickest end of the bat.

Defensive magic poured out of my palm, crackling with heat as it circled the barrel. I concentrated, forcing the magic out until it fully enveloped the business side of my weapon. When I released my hold on the magic, it sank into the wood like a cloth absorbing water and disappeared.

My bat now looked ordinary to anyone who couldn't sense it, but the magic would make it feel like shards of broken glass were embedded into the smooth wood. The intruder had no idea what he was in for.

I gripped the bat at the thinnest end, letting the midsection rest on my shoulder as I reached for the door-knob with my other hand and steeled myself for this confrontation. *Think like a wolf, Shiloh. Defend your territory.*

On a silent count of three, I yanked the door open and burst into the bar. Both hands gripped the bat while I hovered it over my shoulder, eyes darting around for my target to strike.

He was male alright, and a werewolf. He was also

stupidly calm for having a pissed-off bar owner coming at him with a bat. In fact, he wasn't even looking at me.

The intruder was looking down, fiddling with a small black contraption in his hand. I spotted a lens on the thing. A camera? There were more of them on the bar, with cardboard boxes and wires stretched out all over the place.

"Hey!" I snapped, raising the bat higher.

The werewolf looked up and froze me in place with the palest, icy blue eyes I'd ever seen. "Oh, hey. I need to get into your cable closet. Is it back there?" He jerked his chin toward the storage room I'd just come out of.

The question, his bored tone, his eyes. None of it made sense. It was all noise in my brain. I stared at him, bewildered. "What?"

"Cable closet. It looks like a little cabinet in the wall, kind of like an electrical panel. It'll have your wireless router, ethernet cables, any phone lines—"

"I know what a cable closet is!" I shouted.

His mouth closed, dark eyebrows furrowing over those eyes that looked more animal than human. Like *he* was the one with the right to be confused.

"And no, you can't get into it. You shouldn't be here at all. We're fucking closed." I tightened my grip on the bat, which the werewolf appeared to notice for the first time.

"Take it easy," he said, lifting a hand. "Your front door was unlocked."

"That's not an invitation!" I screeched.

He frowned, jaw muscles ticking under the dark beard that coated his jaw. "Why else would you leave it unlocked?"

"Because I have to carry trash to the dumpsters! Why am I even having this conversation with you?"

"I dunno, *you* came out here with a weapon to yell at me."

"You broke into my bar!"

"I did not, your fucking door was unlocked!"

"Fucking moon, are you really this dense?" Now I really wanted to swing the bat. Not at him, necessarily, but just to hit something so I could let this frustration out. "Why are you even here?"

He pointed to the boxes and wires laid out on the bar. "Installing security cameras. What does it look like?"

I stared at him, my confusion only growing. "I never asked for security cameras."

"The alpha said I was to install them." The wolf's expression relaxed with a realization dawning on him. "I guess he never told you."

He definitely did not. My focal point up until then had only been the wolf's eyes because they were so unusually bright. Now that I figured out he wasn't going to rob or hurt me, I took in the rest of him.

He wore a black leather vest over a snug white T-shirt that hugged around his biceps. The patch on the left side of the vest was a wolf's skull, jaws open and ready to strike. A symbol I and all of Vargmore knew well. On the back of the vest, I knew that same skull would be a large centerpiece framed by the words HOWLING DEATH MC.

The biker club of werewolves was also the reigning pack of Vargmore, and this fucking know-it-all was part of them?

"You're with Howling Death?" I asked skeptically.

The wolf glanced down at his patch as if to make sure it was still there. "Yeah."

"And it was Derric who sent you to install security cameras in my bar?"

"Yeah," he repeated.

I cocked my head as I stared at him. I thought I knew of every wolf in Howling Death, but I would definitely remember those eyes if I had seen them before. "What's your name?"

"Orson," he said. "I'm the treasurer and tech security for the pack."

"How come I've never seen you before?"

Orson shrugged. "Don't go out much."

Yeah, that much was obvious, what with the whole inviting himself in and not even bothering to introduce himself display.

Might as well lead by example. "Well, I'm Shiloh."

"I know. Your name's on the business license and all the financial records of the bar."

It's called being polite, asshole, but okay, nevermind.

"Well, I'm sorry you had to come out all this way." I forced a smile through gritted teeth. "But I will not be having security cameras in my establishment."

Orson's brows slashed down again, his eyes hardening like tempered glass. "Yes, you will. That's what I'm here to do."

Hoo boy. Was I really going to have to spell it out for him? "Derric never consulted me about this. So I'm not consenting to cameras until he explains his reasoning to me."

"He is the *alpha*," Orson argued.

"And this is *my* business," I retorted.

Orson's arm shot out toward the front door. "A vampire walked in here last month with a gun, damaged the property, and injured two people. You're less than a mile from the border and you *don't* want added security?"

"I don't want people coming in here and fucking with *my* business without my knowledge or consent." I crossed my arms, still holding my enchanted baseball bat. "Please take your things and leave."

"I don't understand you," Orson said with a shake of his head. "This is for your protection. For the protection of your customers and every citizen that lives here."

"Tell the alpha to call me," I said. "If this is so important, he can talk to me and I'll consider it. But you can't just break in here after business hours—"

"The door was unlocked!"

"I don't give a FUCK!" My boiling point had been reached, and I was beyond done talking in circles with this pedantic furball. "Get out, just get the fuck out of here."

"Stubborn witch," the werewolf snarled as he began throwing everything into one cardboard box with more force than necessary. From the inhuman rumble of his growl, and his canines elongating, I knew his animal half was near the surface. It happened sometimes when werewolves couldn't get a grip on their emotions. The guy was pissed, like he had any right to be. Like *I* was the one being unreasonable.

It was nowhere near the full moon, so there was no reason for him to lose control of his animal. But then again, I didn't know this particular werewolf. How was I to know if he was stable, feral, or simply an asshole prone to violence? For that reason, I tightened my grip on the bat and lifted it higher.

Orson gave me a bored look as he pulled his box of camera equipment off the bar. "Relax, I'm leaving. For the fucking moon's sake, I was just trying to help."

"Great. Here's a tip you should have learned as a pup." I brought the bat down next to my leg and brought my opposite hand to my hip. "Ask permission first. Before you do literally anything that involves another person. It'll get you a lot farther."

The werewolf only gave a dismissive snort as he went out the door without another word. No goodbye, goodnight, sorry to bother you, or even a middle finger thrown back at me. I could only stare in the direction he left, processing the interaction we'd just had.

"What a rude fucking asshole," I declared to the empty room.

The more I replayed our conversation in my head, the more pissed off I became, to the point where I was fuming. How did someone make it to adulthood with an attitude like this? Surely he would've been smacked by elders as a pup for mouthing off like that. Surely he didn't speak like that to Derric, the alpha of the whole territory, who commanded respect.

Was it because I was a woman? Or a witch? Or was I the problem?

With a resigned sigh, I dragged the bat behind me as I returned to the storage room. Truth be told, I was already emotionally raw, a little touchy, even before Orson stepped foot inside the bar.

After Sawyer ended things with us, I did my best to move on with my head up high and a smile on my face. Break-ups happened. We could be mature about it. To his credit, he did his best to be honest without being cruel. He didn't string me along and lie about having deeper feelings than he really had. We weren't even together for that long. It should have been easy to move on from him.

Too bad I fell way harder in those few weeks than I ever intended. I didn't even realize it until he broke it off. And when he found his mate, who turned out to be a latent shifter herself, so soon after? That was just salt, vinegar, and some barbed wire in the wound.

Werewolves had this allure about them, a kind of romantic mystery, even though I'd grown up and spent my whole life around them. They were all incredibly attractive by human and witch standards. Sometimes they dated and married us non-shifters, but that happened rarely. Werewolf packs and families were so tightly knit that they usually stuck to mating their own kind. So they were usually unattainable to people like me.

Sure they were my neighbors, friends, acquaintances, and customers. But by and large they kept to themselves, which only reinforced that mysteriousness. Even the gentlest, most soft-spoken werewolves I knew had a wildness about them that was fascinating.

So when Sawyer, Howling Death's enforcer, started flirting with me, I couldn't believe my luck. But as it turned out, I couldn't measure up after all.

The fact that Orson had just waltzed in here and started setting up like *he* owned the place instead of me reinforced the idea that I didn't matter. I was just in the way, a distraction. Like I didn't deserve the same respect because I couldn't howl at the moon and run on four legs. If I had been a wolf, I was damn sure Orson would have knocked first. His scruff would have been between my teeth otherwise.

I couldn't blame Sawyer, of course. Our incompatibilities went beyond our biology. But feelings weren't always rational, and right then, they were a big, swirling mess.

I definitely blamed Orson for being an asshole though. And whenever the Howling Death alpha deigned to call me up, I would give him a piece of my mind about his treasurer. Hopefully he'd teach that wolf some basic manners.

Orson wasn't even hot enough to get away with being rude. Sure, he had that big, powerful body, but those arctic eyes of his were freaky. Not sexy at all. The dark hair and sharp jawline with a short beard? Didn't do it for me in the slightest. Nope, not one bit.

After returning my bat to its corner behind the door, I only got through one more box of inventory before I heard a loud *slam*. Like someone had swung the front door open so hard, it slammed into the wall.

"Are you fucking kidding me?" My anger that had simmered down returned to a boiling rage. That werewolf had some fucking nerve.

I marched for the storage room door and shoved it open. Only one person could slam door around here and that was me, asshole.

"Didn't I fucking tell you—"

I stopped short at the sight of the man across the bar, who was not Orson.

He wasn't even a werewolf.

This man wore a long, dusty brown coat and equally dusty boots. His eyes were even stranger than Orson's because they were bright orange and had a long vertical pupil like a reptile's. On top of that, those eyes were sinister and cunning.

"Sorry, we're closed." All my internal alarms were going off, and I tried my best to sound firm with this stranger, despite the unease coiling through me.

The man only gave me the creepiest smile I'd ever seen, revealing extended canines. A rippling, shimmer effect ran over the side of his face, and a stripe of bright orange scales appeared from his cheekbone to his jaw.

I became prey, frozen in place. Every instinct screamed at me to run, but my muscles locked up. Besides, where could I run to? This dragon shifter could torch the entire building, and me in it, if he so much as sneezed.

As if the scales on his face weren't enough proof as to what he was, a set of wide, leathery wings spread out from his back. Watching those limbs grow and fan out would have been beautiful, fascinating even, if I wasn't so damn terrified.

With one beat of his wings, the dragon shifter kicked up a gust that whipped back my hair, sent receipts and invoices flying, and swung the front door shut.

"Have a seat, witch," he said in a low, gravelly voice. "You and I have a lot to talk about."

CHAPTER 2

SHILOH

Damn it, why did I leave my phone in the back room? I needed to alert Sawyer, Derric, hell, the entire Howling Death pack right fucking *now*.

As allies of the vampires, dragon shifters were forbidden from coming into Vargmore. All of the territory's residents, werewolves and humans alike, were forbidden from associating with dragons or vampires.

This dragon was risking all-out war by coming to my bar and cornering me. And holy shit, I did *not* want to be at the center of such a conflict.

"There's nothing for us to talk about." I hid the shaking in my voice as best I could. "I don't mean to be rude, but for the safety of both of our territories, I have to ask you to leave."

"Oh, don't be like that, little witch." He approached the bar and set his hands on the surface. Each finger was covered in orange-gold scales and tipped with long black claws. Fuck, this guy didn't even need to breathe fire to kill me. "You can help me *immensely*."

"I refuse."

The dragon cocked his head at me, his creepy smile getting wider. "I'm afraid that's not an option."

"I won't betray my territory!"

He lunged across the bar, the movement faster than my eyes could track. A cold grip wrapped around my forearm and pulled me forward so hard, I thought my arm might rip out of the socket.

"No! Let me go!" I tried to pull back, but my strength was no match for the dragon shifter. My enchanted baseball bat flashed through my mind, and I lifted my free hand, ready to hurl some defensive magic straight into his face.

I never got the chance to before he scraped a dark claw over my wrist and the back of my hand in his grip. The scratch burned so badly, my mind went empty of everything except the pain.

When I tried to pull away again, he released me so abruptly that I went flailing backwards until the counter hit me in the center of my back. I sank to the floor and curled up, hot tears burning down my face, my back and arm throbbing as I whimpered for this dragon shifter to not kill me.

"That mark will not go away until you've fulfilled what I need." He nodded at the scratch he made, which became a long, ugly stripe surrounded by red, irritated skin. "So, are you ready to talk?"

I looked down at his mark. The skin was raised and black, textured in what looked like hard scales. And it hurt so fucking badly.

"What do you want?" I whispered, cradling my arm to my chest.

"I need a potion made in a fairly large amount." He smiled again, forearms on the bar like he was just another customer ordering a drink. "That's your specialty, isn't it, little witch?"

"Don't you have witches in your own territory?" I shot back. "Why bring me into this?"

"We have our sun witches, yes, but they're of no use for this particular potion." His reptilian eyes fixated on me. "The ingredients I need are in Vargmore's forests."

It took all of my energy to stay composed. All I wanted to do was writhe around and scream, maybe stick my arm in an ice bath for this burning pain. I could barely get my thoughts together, but I *needed* to. I needed to be smart about this.

Right then, it felt like the only smart thing to do was be compliant with his demands, and maybe this pain would let up. He couldn't stay in the territory forever, so the moment he was gone, I would call up Howling Death.

"What's the potion?" My eyes stung and I blinked, realizing just then how much I was sweating.

"Visakari's Kiss."

Oh fuck no. No, no, no.

"That's impossible," I said with a shake of my head. "The main ingredient is extinct."

"I'm sure you have dried specimens somewhere. You moon witches like to keep your collections."

"Even if we did, I'm not sure how viable they would be."

"Then propagate them so you have fresh specimens. I don't care what you do, but I need a gallon of it."

"A *gallon*?!" I stared at him, wondering if he had any idea of the impossibility he was asking for. "No one has ever made that much. Even when the silver deadnettle wasn't extinct, the most that could ever be extracted was *maybe* a tablespoon."

"Then it sounds like you have a lot of work ahead of

you. Best get to it." He leaned up from the bar as if to leave, then stopped. "Oh, and if you breathe a word of this to anyone, especially Howling Death, I'll rain fire upon this whole fucking territory." That creepy smile returned. "Just make the potion for me and all will be well, little witch. I'll be back in a few days to check in."

"A few days isn't anywhere near long enough," I protested. "That recipe will take weeks. And in the amount you want, it could take months."

"I don't have that kind of time. And neither do you, so make it happen." He tapped his wrist. "Tick tock, little witch."

He left with that, and only after his heavy footsteps crossed the room and the door closed behind him, did it become slightly easier to breathe.

Not by much though.

The pain in my arm ebbed slightly, like now that he was farther away, his mark had calmed down.

I stared at the long ugly line burned into my skin. Would he be able to sense me like this? Track my movement or even my emotions? Werewolves were said to be able to sense each others' mates through mating bites. Was this the dragon equivalent of that?

Oh dear moon, if this dragon shifter had made me his fucking mate, I was going to be sick.

My first thought was I'd have to look for a spell to get the mark removed. But no, he would sense that, wouldn't he? And if he was crazy enough to cross into enemy territory, mark me without consent, and threaten all of Vargmore?

I believed without a doubt that he would carry out his promise to set fire to the territory, and that was terrifying.

So it seemed I had no choice but to make this impossible, and also incredibly dangerous, potion for him.

Fuck me.

One thought kept lingering as I cleaned up my spilled papers, my frazzled brain trying to return to normalcy in the face of the bizarre and terrifying evening.

As much I hated to admit it, I wished Orson hadn't left so quickly.

CHAPTER 3
ORSON

After that bar owner witch, Shiloh, kicked me out last night, I knew exactly what to do. She didn't want security cameras inside? No problem. I'd just install them *outside*. She owned the business within the building, but not the trees outside of it.

I'd need slightly different equipment for the install, but all it took was switching some things out and I was golden.

Who knew what that witch's deal was? Not me. I had a job to do. The alpha told me to do something, so I would do it. It wasn't my fault that she got all bent out of shape because I didn't call ahead first.

Granted, I didn't know I was supposed to call ahead. Put that on the long list of things that I didn't magically know beforehand.

I was rummaging through my supply closet at the Howling Death lodge when a knock came on the jamb. Looking over my shoulder, I nodded at the large werewolf filling up the doorway. "Hey, Tryn."

"You're up early," he observed.

"Yeah," I confirmed, returning to scanning the shelves.

He didn't leave nor did he say anything else, so I just kept gathering up the equipment I needed while my pack-mate stood there.

I wasn't one for small talk, or really talking in general. For one thing, I wasn't good at it. For another, it was boring and trite. I figured it was one of the main reasons why I preferred numbers and technology. Those things were straightforward. Once you knew formulas and how things worked, they just made sense.

People didn't make sense, no matter how hard I tried.

And that witch, Shiloh, was the most nonsensical of all.

"What are you up to?" Tryn finally asked.

"Gonna install some surveillance for Stout & Spirit."

"I thought you did that last night?"

"I tried, but the owner got mad and told me to leave."

"Aw geez, Orson." When I turned around, Tryn had a hand on his face. "What did you say to her?"

"Nothing," I growled. "Besides telling her what I was there to do. She went off and started yelling, saying I broke into her place even though her door was unlocked."

"Why would she do that?"

"Hell if I know."

Tryn crossed his thick arms, eyeballing me like a parent lecturing a pup. "Well, did you *ask* her if you could do the install?"

"Well no, but—"

"It's pretty important to ask first, Orson."

"Derric told me to do the install, so that's what I went to do!" Frustration roughened my voice and I could feel my wolf getting agitated. He was snapping his jaws, feeling defensive and cornered, his hackles raised.

"Take it easy," Tryn growled in warning. "I'm not attacking you, just trying to help you learn this stuff."

"You might as well give up," I snarled. "It's just not sticking."

There were so many rules to communicating with others, and none of them were consistent for every situation. I could walk into the lodge and grab a drink and food from the kitchen without asking anyone, but I couldn't do that at Stout & Spirit. Usually, there were no problems when the alpha gave me an order and I obeyed, but this time, there was. For every rule, there was an exception, and I couldn't keep it all straight. There was no formula to dealing with others, which was why I avoided most people outside my pack.

Aside from Sawyer's mate, Riley, I was the wolf most recently initiated into Howling Death. And it came not long after my introduction to a non-feral society in general.

Tryn came up to me and clamped a large hand on the back of my neck. "I'm not giving up on you, Orson. We're packmates. You're my brother. I know it's frustrating, but you'll learn this stuff. It's not easy, even for people who are well socialized."

I shook my head with a big sigh. Derric may have been the alpha, but Tryn was the glue which held the pack together. He was everyone's friend, and genuinely so. I knew he was sincerely trying to help me, not blowing smoke up my ass. He also had some witch blood in him and seemed to know things beyond what his keen wolf senses told him. I just wished he'd be able to see that I was a lost cause.

"So you're trying this install again," he said, clapping me on the shoulder before dropping his hand. "What are you doing differently?"

"I'm putting a few cameras in the trees to watch the front door and exterior of the bar," I answered.

Tryn closed his eyes, tilting his head back, and I knew I'd answered wrong. Again.

"I was hoping you'd say you were apologizing to Shiloh and asking permission this time."

"Apologize for what?"

"I know you've got more than two brain cells in there, Ors. Use 'em."

Another growl of frustration rumbled out of my chest before I could stop it. "I have no idea what I'm supposed to apologize for. I just did what the alpha told me."

"Here's a tip for you, pup." It was almost word-for-word what Shiloh had said to me, which made me even more annoyed. "The trick to getting along with people is having empathy. Put yourself in *her* shoes. Think about it from *her* perspective. Imagine how it would feel from her side of the conversation. Make sense?"

"Sure." I shoved the last piece of equipment into my backpack. "I'll see you later, Tryn." He thankfully moved out of the doorway and I made my escape.

A few of my packmates were lounging in the common room, and I nodded good morning to them as I crossed the expansive space. See? My packmates weren't complicated. Why did everything else have to be?

Pushing through the heavy front door, I crossed the lodge's wraparound porch in two long strides before coming up to my motorcycle. I turned on the machine and it broke through the quiet morning like a massive beast awaking from its slumber. It was no wonder why us shifters liked riding so much. A motorcycle was the one vehicle that seemed just as much animal as machine.

I walked the bike backward, just far enough to turn, and then settled in for the ride. There were lots of things I had to learn when I came into the Howling Death pack.

The worst? Socializing. The best? Riding, one hundred percent.

The morning air was crisp as it rushed over my skin. The last of the fog was burning off as the sun began to rise. I actually liked running through Vargmore's forests on cold, foggy mornings. It reminded me of the better times before I'd joined the pack, the best part of being feral. The world was quietest at that time, heavy with magic, especially after a full moon.

But on this morning, I had a job to do. I wanted to install these cameras before Stout & Spirit opened for business and definitely before Shiloh woke up to yell at me again.

Something I couldn't properly express the night before, and I still didn't fully understand, was that I *needed* to protect Shiloh. These cameras needed to go up because she needed to be safe. And *I* had to be the one who kept her safe.

All throughout our arguing last night, my wolf was howling inside me and clawing to come out. Not because he was angry with her, that was all my human side. But because he wanted to stand guard over her, watch for any threats against her, dispose of them with his teeth and claws, then lay them at her feet.

It was mostly to appease him, this sneaking out to put cameras in the trees, because it was one step closer to making her safer. That was my wolf's number one priority ever since last night, and it threw me for one hell of a loop.

My wolf was skittish. Withdrawn. Still feral by most civilized werewolf standards. The only time he reacted to anything was when he felt threatened. Otherwise, he was often silent and unseen.

That all changed last night when we went into Stout &

Spirit for the first time, where Shiloh's scent filled the space. And at the first whiff of it, my wolf became a goddamn golden retriever.

His tail wagged like a windshield wiper on the fastest speed. He was full-on grinning, paws tapping the ground in a happy little dance. He wanted to roll over and show her his belly, lick her face, and feel her scratch his ears.

It was like the moon herself had extracted my wolf from my soul and replaced it with a completely different one. The human side of me was just along for the ride and saying, "What the fuck?" the whole time. I mean sure, Shiloh *did* have a nice natural scent. It was fresh citrus with a bit of spice, something like cinnamon.

I had never been interested in hooking up with females before. Sure, I repeated some crass jokes that my packmates said, but actually doing it took a level of social skills I did not have. But with my wolf having a personality transplant and that sweet scent, I thought I might be interested in getting to know this witch, who everyone seemed to know and love.

That was until she burst out of her back room, wielding a baseball bat, and accused me of breaking in, despite knowing full well the front door was unlocked.

Imagine how it would feel from her side of the conversation. Tryn's words echoed through my head, a calming force in my swirling maelstrom of thoughts.

Fear had begun tainting her scent last night, moments before she confronted me with the bat. She had been afraid of me, and I recalled how my wolf took great personal offense. His excited yips had turned into distressed whines and then mournful howls. He felt...rejected. Hurt. He wanted her joy, not her fear. That was what spurred his protective instincts into overdrive too. My animal was determined to make her fear go away, and to do that, we had to make her safe.

Even more oddly, the sight of her with that baseball bat had excited him. We both saw the hardened expression on her face framed by silky black hair, the narrowed sage green eyes, and the flushed skin highlighting the freckles on her nose.

My wolf was giving me such whiplash, the first thing that came out of my mouth was stupidly asking about her cable closet. Even someone as socially stunted as me knew that I was supposed to say hello and introduce myself. But I had no chance to backtrack and didn't want to look like an idiot in front of her anyway. For some reason, that had been important to me. And Shiloh was already pissed off at me at that point.

Damn it, now I was starting to see why. My wolf had been yelling at me to do one thing while Shiloh was afraid and wanted me to do the exact opposite. She had no idea what was going on with me though. How could she? We had never met before.

I was way out of my element and handled the whole thing poorly. I handled most conversations poorly, but letting Shiloh down felt like an especially bad offense.

We have to make it right. My wolf was determined, his ears erect, eyes sharp, and snout pointed straight in the direction of Shiloh's bar.

"How?" The sound of the word was lost, taken by the wind rushing past me on the road. But it wasn't like I needed the sound to carry. I was essentially talking to myself.

Protect her, my wolf growled.

〉〉〉〉〉〉〉〉〉〉〉〉〉〉〉〉

I PARKED a few hundred yards away from Stout & Spirit and walked the rest of the way so that my bike wouldn't rouse anyone at this early hour. The bar looked like a charming cabin from the outside, with a slate roof and red-bricked chimney. The building itself too looked like it was sleeping, all quiet and still before waking up with its cozy interior lights and all the conversations and people to energize it.

Definitely not my scene.

I had a fleeting thought of going to Shiloh's apartment above the bar, knocking and properly asking to do the install this time. And also maybe apologizing for how I acted. The very thought of potentially making her angry again, and first thing in the morning, made my palms sweaty, so that was a no-go. Besides, everything I brought with me was specifically for my tree-surveillance idea.

I walked the treeline directly across from the bar, figuring out the best vantage point. The trees needed to have a good view of the front door and also be densely covered enough to hide the camera lens.

There was no need to point a camera at the back side, I figured. Besides, the entrance to Shiloh's apartment was back there, and she deserved the privacy. I wasn't here to be a creep.

Why *was* I here though? If she knew I put cameras in the trees, she'd be doubly pissed.

We must protect her, my wolf insisted with a bark.

"Yeah, yeah," I muttered before I settled on a tree and proceeded to climb.

I told myself I was continuing to follow my alphas orders, which was to set up surveillance at a vulnerable spot near our territory's border. Making my wolf shut up about Shiloh was just an added bonus. Two birds, one stone.

Once settled between two thick branches of the tree, I started setting up. The camera would be powered by a small solar panel and also had a battery back-up if the panel were to fail for some reason. I fixed everything in place with some zip ties and duct tape with a tree bark pattern for camouflage. Once everything was secure, I tested the livestreaming function through an app I'd designed on my phone. After playing with the camera angle for a bit, I decided it was good enough and climbed down from the tree.

I walked backwards toward the bar, keeping my eyes on the tree to make sure the camera wouldn't be visible. As I neared the building, a mix of odd scents hit my nose. I inhaled deeply, frowning. I smelled...something burnt? That definitely wasn't there last night. Although maybe Shiloh had cooked dinner for herself after I left and had kept it in the oven too long.

But there was something else too. I lifted my face to scent the air again and got hit in the face with the familiar smell of her fear. Only this wasn't like last night. It was far more potent and mixed with a salty quality, like sweat.

Or tears.

I turned to face the building, staring at the front door like it had all the answers. When I tried the knob, it was, of course, locked.

My wolf went nuts again, howling in despair. His paws dug and scraped so hard from underneath my skin, I felt tangible pain on my sternum and ribs.

We have wronged her. We must make it right!

"No." I rubbed my chest in an attempt to soothe my animal. "Something else happened here." I remembered clearly last night that Shiloh was more pissed off than scared. And she definitely wasn't crying or sweating.

That only set my wolf off even more. His fur spiked up, hackles raised, and teeth fully on display. He wasn't a defensive, skittish thing anymore, but in full-on attack mode. My wolf wanted to go to war for Shiloh.

We must protect our witch. Find who made her cry and lay their corpse at her feet.

"Okay, no. We need to leave."

I headed for my bike, despite all the howling and growling rattling around my brain. Wait, shit. That growling wasn't just in my head but coming from my throat.

My wolf and I were separate entities, but because we shared a soul, there was significant overlap between him and me. While in human form, I had control and could usually rein him in. When shifted, it was the reverse. And during the night of the full moon, the wolf was the only driver.

So it was really fucking weird that he was having this much influence over me when it came to Shiloh. His instinct to protect her was becoming my own. His desire to lay waste to anyone that would harm her made me want to beat a man to death with my bare fists. And when he called her *our* witch, I had the strangest urge to call her *my* witch.

It made no fucking sense. I didn't even know Shiloh. She definitely didn't know me.

And the cherry on top? She most likely hated me, so what was even the point?

CHAPTER 4

SHILOH

I had hoped it was all a nightmare. Just a bad dream.

My eyes weren't even open when I felt the throbbing ache in my arm the next morning. I went to touch the raised mark and nearly cried out. It no longer felt like a burning hot brand, but it was hypersensitive to any kind of touch. My own fingers felt like broken glass dragging over an open wound.

Rolling upright, I was careful not to brush my arm against the sheets. The dragon's harsh voice repeated in my mind. *I'll rain fire on your whole fucking territory.* He'd said it so casually and with that creepy smile. I knew in my gut it wasn't an empty threat. Dragons were dangerous and conniving on the best of days. This guy, whoever he was, was on another level, and that was straight up terrifying.

The safety of the entire territory was on *my* shoulders now. And to keep it safe, I had to make an extremely volatile potion, with extinct ingredients, that probably hadn't been made in the last thousand years. Oh, and I had to make a fucking gallon of it.

I brought my hands to my face, rubbing my eyes with a

groan. All I wanted to do was tell Derric. Let the were-wolves handle it. This was why Howling Death was the reigning pack, to protect everyone else against the dragons and the vampires.

But would this dragon know?

My arm continued to ache and throb, a constant reminder of last night. Not like I needed the reminder, that horrible scene kept playing over and over in my head.

"Fuck." I let the back of my head hit the headboard. There was truly no way out of this that I could see. Not one that wasn't too risky.

The sound of beating wings outside my window sent my heart racing. Sweet moon, he was back *already*?

I scrambled to the corner of the wall, hissing at the pain of my arm scraping against the bed sheets. Still, I pulled the blankets up to my chin and tried to make myself as small as possible.

"Hey Shiloh, you up?" called a familiar voice. "I got my hands full, can't knock."

I sagged with relief and almost laughed at myself. Of course, those were the feathered wings of an angel beating outside my door. Not the scales and skin of a dragon.

"Give me a minute, Kaz!" I yelled before climbing out of bed.

It took a lot of gritting my teeth and fighting back tears to pull a blouse on over the mark. Then I hunted in my bathroom for something to wrap around my arm, because regular ol' band-aids weren't going to do it. I settled for just wrapping my arm in gauze for the time being, again biting against the pain of the fabric pressing on the mark.

When I opened the front door, Kaz was still hovering in mid-air, his wings keeping a steady beat to stay elevated. It was impressive, considering he was holding a keg in each hand, presumably full of beer.

"You never get tired of showing off, do you?" I grinned, leaning against the jamb.

He shrugged, another impressive feat with the weight on each of his hands. "It's a good wing workout."

"Uh-huh." I started down the stairs while he steadily dropped in altitude to keep up with me.

The kegs touched the ground when I did, and then Kaz's booted feet followed. He rolled his wrists, the veins popping in his tattooed forearms. His rust-colored wings tucked in closer to his back now that they were no longer in use.

"Gonna feel light as a feather when I fly home," he said, stretching his arms above his head.

"I bet." I leaned over to inspect the kegs. "So what do you got for me?"

"A gruit, which I believe your witch clientèle would like." He touched one finger to the first keg's cap, then the other. "And my favorite. A red ale, for the autumnal season coming up."

"Great, I'll put it on during the equinox," I said, heading for my cold storage. "I got clean empties for you."

Just when I started to think about how nice it was to be distracted by regular work talk, Kaz asked, "Are you okay, Shiloh?"

"Yeah, of course!" I said, making my voice more chipper while avoiding eye contact as I unlocked things. "Why do you ask?"

"You just seem a little on edge, that's all."

Damn angels and their empathic abilities to sense emotions.

"Just a long night." I held up my bandaged arm for a

second before returning it close to my body. "Little accident with a broken glass, that's all."

"Oh shit. Well, don't move that stuff. I got it." Kaz darted into my cold box, effectively blocking me from going in with that wingspan of his. In the work of a moment, he removed my empty kegs and brought in the two new ones he just flew over.

"Thanks," I muttered.

To say angels were chivalrous by nature was an understatement. Some believed their old-fashioned ways were misogynistic, and in some practices, that might have been true. I heard that female angels were put on a pedestal, quite literally. They were revered as precious, almost sacred beings, but that came with a lot of archaic restrictions such as never being able to leave the territory without a male escort.

Those were the rumors, at least. Despite working with Kaz's brewery since my bar opened, I'd never spent much time in Helios City, the angel territory which was also a huge, sprawling metropolis. I preferred the wildness of Vargmore. Every rock, animal, and blade of grass here was a sponge, absorbing the moon's magic. The same magic that beat through me and awoke the beasts of the werewolves.

In the few times I visited Helios City, I felt cut off from my magic. I might as well have my sense of taste or smell removed. So, my visits to the angel territory were few and far between. Usually they were business trips to Kaz's brewery, so it wasn't all bad.

"There you go, all set." Kaz closed everything back up with a warm smile. He was a rare kind of angel, one who didn't mind physical labor and getting his hands dirty. That was probably why he ran the only brewery in Helios City. Good thing he was a masterful brewer as well.

"Thank you, Kaz. You didn't have to——"

He waved that away. "You really should hire some muscle rather than do all this switching out yourself."

My eyes narrowed at him. "I'm stronger than I look, *Kazath*."

"I know." He laughed. "You don't have to say my full name like my mother. But you do need extra help running this place. I've been telling you for years."

"I do have someone starting tonight, actually." With all the drama from last night, I'd forgotten I'd be starting Riley today.

Yeah, my ex's new mate who was impossible to not love.

"Oh good." Kaz crossed his arms, beaming down at me from his ridiculous height. "Didn't I tell you Stout & Spirit would only get busier as time went on?"

"You did," I admitted. "I didn't believe you, but you were right."

His gaze changed for a split second. It was so fast I almost didn't catch it. His expression seemed to become... heated. Like this was not just a friendly chat between two business owners.

And just as quickly, it was gone. Kaz broke eye contact to look all around the receiving bay we were in. "I'm really proud of you, Shiloh. It took a lot more than magic to get this place off the ground."

"What can I say?" I affectionately tapped the door of the cold box. "She's my baby."

The angel chuckled, his wings rustling slightly. "You've done amazingly well as a single mother." He turned to face me and that heated look returned. "But you don't have to do it alone, you know."

My breath came up short. Whatever he was hinting at, I did not have the time or mental bandwidth to deal with it.

"I gotta get ready to open up," I said, sliding past him. "Invoice me for those kegs and I'll pay them tonight."

)))))) ● (((((

"What's a..a *groot*?"

"Gruit," I corrected Riley, who was studying my sheet of beer styles. It was a slower night at Stout & Spirit, which was perfect for her to learn the ropes. "It's a beer that's bittered with herbs instead of hops. It's a very old style, one that witches tend to love."

"That's so cool." She turned the sheet over, scanning the extensive list. "I didn't know there were so many styles."

"We rotate, but usually only have four or five on at a time." I gestured to the beer taps mounted on the wall. "So these are the only ones you need to know for now."

"How do you decide which ones to carry?"

"I usually just take what Kaz gives me," I admitted. "Everything he makes is spectacular. If there's a high demand for something, I'll request more of that, but as you've seen," I turned and looked out at the serving area, "almost everyone is happy to take what we have and try something new."

"Sawyer loves the IPA." Riley made a face. "It's too bitter for me though."

Absolutely nothing passed through me at the mention of my kind-of-ex boyfriend, which was a relief. "Try the gruit," I suggested. "I think you'll like it."

Riley did a few taste tests and practiced her beer-pouring, while I stuck with the more complicated cocktails and woodfire pizza orders. Okay, maybe Kaz had a point. This was already a hundred times easier with one extra pair of hands.

In the time that I left for and came back from a bathroom break, Riley was carefully pouring a beer for an icy-eyed werewolf that stopped me in my tracks.

Orson's gaze landed on me and didn't leave. Strangely enough, those eyes sent a flush of warmth through me rather than the arctic chill I expected.

"How's this, boss?" Riley glanced over at me as she wiped excess foam from the glass and placed the drink in front of the werewolf.

"Uh, good! That's a perfect pour, Riley." I broke eye contact with Orson and looked around for something to make me busy.

"Opening a tab, Orson?"

I didn't catch his response as Riley went through the usual procedure with him. When I looked up, his broad back faced me as he walked away with his drink, settling into a booth against the wall, by himself.

"Well, that's a first," I muttered, wiping down the bar that didn't need it because Riley had already done so.

"I was just about to say," she chuckled, stacking clean glasses in their designated areas. "He doesn't seem like the type. Every time Sawyer and I are at the lodge, he's always hidden away on a computer."

Sure enough, Orson had pulled a slim laptop and small wireless mouse from his backpack and set up shop on the table. His face was aglow from the screen as he sipped his drink.

I hadn't expected to see him again, much less as a

customer. If he were to come back here at all, I'd figured it would be to apologize for acting like an absolute dick.

But time ticked by and of course, that didn't happen. Orson just continued working alone while nursing his drink. Whatever. He had a right to be here, just like anyone else in Vargmore. A couple more Howling Death were-wolves came in, and they spoke to Orson briefly but didn't join him at his table.

"He's really kind of a loner, huh?" I was filling a flat of glassware for the dishwasher and hoped my staring wasn't too obvious. "Even for being in the pack."

"Yeah, Orson kind of keeps to himself." Riley was studying my beer sheet again. "I think he's just really intro-verted. Sawyer says he gets really uncomfortable when he has to talk to people for an extended period of time. He's always been really polite to me though."

"If only we all could be so lucky," I muttered, pushing the back door open with a pop of my hip.

"Oh, let me get that!" Riley rushed over to hold the door for me.

"Thanks. Can you tell I'm not used to having help?"

"It's what I'm here for," she said cheerily.

Again, impossible to hate such a sweet girl.

At closing time, Orson had just finished nursing his first and only beer. Once he set down the empty glass, he closed his laptop and began putting things away. Moments later, he came up to the bar with his empty glass in hand.

"I'll get you closed out right here, Orson." Riley went to the register in front of him, fingers flying over the screen, when her mate came through the door. "Oh hey, babe! One sec."

"Take your time," Sawyer drawled. He clapped Orson

on the back as he approached, and Orson gave him a curt nod in return.

I didn't know what propelled my feet forward, or what prompted the words to come out of my mouth, but I came up next to Riley and said, "I'll close him out. You two love-birds get going."

Riley hesitated, even though she clearly wanted nothing more than to be on her mate's motorcycle, wrapped around his broad body and heading home. "Are you sure? It'll only take a second."

"Yeah, I got it." I gave her shoulder a little squeeze. "You did great today. Thanks for all your help."

"Thanks, Shiloh! I had fun." Riley shouldered her purse and gave me a quick hug on her way out. "Same time tomorrow?"

"Sure. It'll probably be busier, but you'll have no problems."

"Can't wait."

Sawyer rapped his knuckles on the bar. "Thanks for taking care of my girl, Shiloh." The gratitude in his expression spoke volumes, way more than his words did. Riley had been through an unimaginable amount of trauma before she and Sawyer could settle into their lives as mates. The whole territory was glad to see her thriving. And I was more than happy to add a sense of normalcy to her life with a job and friendship.

For the second time, I was relieved to feel nothing but a warm glow when Sawyer spoke to me. I truly was over him, thank the moon. And the happiness I felt for him and his mate was genuine.

"Anytime," I told him. "Besides, she's kind of my girl now too."

The werewolf enforcer's laugh was tinged with a low

growl as he tucked his mate against his side, his arm resting over her shoulders. "I'll fight you for her, witch."

"No fighting." Riley slapped a palm to his chest. "Or I'll have you banned from the bar."

I cackled. "See? *My* girl."

They turned to leave, Sawyer playfully grumbling while Riley continued to tease him. And then it was just me and Orson, who waited with a blank expression on the other side of the register.

"Sorry for the wait." I pulled up his tab and printed out the receipt in a moment's work.

"Not a problem," he muttered, accepting a pen as he pulled out his wallet and stared down at the bill for his one beer.

He seemed to be taking some time with it, thumbing through his wallet and scribbling on the receipt. A lot of work to pay for a single drink, but whatever. I busied myself with taking another flat of glassware to the dishwasher. In the few seconds I spent in the back room, loading the machine, starting another cycle, and then re-emerging behind the bar, Orson had left.

Before even looking at his bill, I marched over to the front door and slid the deadbolt into place. Not that it would stop that psycho dragon shifter, but I was just following instincts. My heart was already pounding, the emptiness of my bar feeling like a vast cavern. Shit, would I ever feel comfortable being alone in this place again?

I stood by the door for a while just trying to calm my erratic heartbeat and listen for the sound of beating wings. All I heard was the sound of motorcycles driving away and then silence.

Once I felt slightly more confident that the dragon wasn't showing up anytime soon, I returned to the bar to close out Orson's tab. His receipt was sitting on top of something, most likely a cash tip, but that wasn't what grabbed my attention first.

I picked up the slip of paper he'd signed and also... drawn on?

In the margin of the receipt, he'd done a fast but eerily accurate pen sketch of a wolf, with its head down, ears back, and tail low. Its eyes were looking up, round and puppy-like, as if it was sad or pleading.

Or maybe apologetic?

Setting the paper aside, I looked at what he'd placed underneath, and my eyes went wide.

He'd left a *massive* cash tip. One that would have been generous for ten drinks, and completely outrageous for just one. I didn't even accept tips, for the most part. Some customers left small amounts or didn't take their change, but I set up my pricing structure to pay myself and any employees a fair wage without the need for tips.

Even so, influences from the United States in the human world sometimes bled over into our world. Some customers insisted on it, and it was easier to accept graciously than argue over it.

But this?

This was way too much.

And Orson had to know that, so what the hell was his deal? Did he think this would make up for his behavior the other night?

With a sigh, I counted out what he owed for the drink and put the rest in an envelope. Once I finished my closing duties and shut the lights off, I took the envelope with me to my apartment.

Tomorrow, I would tell him where he could shove his money "apology".

CHAPTER 5
ORSON

I replayed the video in slow motion, not wanting to miss anything. The picture was grainy due to the lack of light and not in color, but it was crisp enough to see who all came in and out of Stout & Spirit last night.

I saw myself park my motorcycle out front and make my way inside. I took note of every face that entered and made sure those exact same people left. Everyone was accounted for, and none of them looked suspicious. I closed out the recording once the bar lights turned off and the light in Shiloh's apartment turned on.

Immediately, I went to the camera's live feed, which showed the bar in real time. The image was sharper now that it was daylight, and Shiloh's car was gone. Probably running errands before opening for business again tonight.

I leaned back in my chair and rubbed the center of my chest where my wolf had been kicking up a storm since we installed the tree cameras.

"There's nothing wrong," I said. "Everything was normal last night."

My animal wasn't satisfied. *She is not safe. Someone has hurt our witch. We must find them.*

"Will you stop calling her that?" I groaned, rubbing my eyes. "She's not ours. She's just a witch that hates me."

She is ours!

You need to stop that, or I'm going to start believing you, I thought in reply.

He was not wrong that she'd been hurt though. Shiloh had a huge white bandage around her arm last night, from her wrist to nearly her elbow. I'd planned to ask about it when I paid for my drink, but she'd been talking to Riley and Sawyer, then got busy with closing up. I didn't want to delay her any longer, plus she didn't seem to want to talk to me anyway.

Also, I'd kind of forgotten everything I wanted to say.

I did want to apologize for the night before, had even practiced and planned what I would say. But once my nose caught that citrus and spice on the air, all the words left so that my head could fill with the scent of her instead.

So I said nothing, as usual.

It was better than being rude, I guess. But she already thought I was, so my Irish goodbye probably didn't make me look any better in her view.

I closed the camera feed and pulled up some Howling Death financial reports, eager to get lost in something that wasn't Shiloh's scent. Or the intensity of her eyes when she was pissed off. Or the fact that she laughed and joked with people who weren't me.

You see? my wolf taunted. *She is ours, and we are hers.*

"Shut up," I grumbled.

Time did fly by once I was able to immerse myself in formulas and number-crunching, then a sharp knock at my door made everything stop. "What?" I growled, spinning in my office chair.

The door opened and Ruse, Howling Death's VP and second in command to the alpha, stuck his head in. "Uh, the owner of Stout & Spirit is here to see *you*." He emphasized that last word like he found it unbelievable that anyone would come see me. And honestly, he was right.

"Shiloh?" I asked dumbly while my wolf pranced happily under my skin.

The other wolf's eyebrows went up. "Oh wow, you even know her name. Really getting out there, huh, Orson?"

"Fuck off, Ruse." I stood up and slid past him, ignoring his self-amused chuckle.

He was a cocky asshole who sniffed Derric's ass too much, but then again, that was probably why he made a good second. What did I know? It wasn't like I had a great sense of character judgment. I had a low-level dislike of just about everyone.

I tried not to inhale too hard as I came down the stairs. Shiloh was waiting in the great room below, and it was like her scent rose up to me, seeking me out. My wolf was so damn happy—no, ecstatic—that she came to see us. His tail whipped back and forth so damn hard, and he wouldn't stop vocalizing, making all kinds of yips and soft barks to greet our mate.

I froze in mid-step, the weight of that thought hitting me like a bowling ball to the gut. *Mate?* Oh, hell no, absolutely not.

You finally see it, my wolf gloated.

Not a chance, furball. Not a snowman's chance in hell.

"Orson?"

Shiloh's voice cut through my panicked mental arguing

and somehow piled on more stress to my senses. She could see me. She was *right there.*

She came to see *me.*

"Sorry, I...just remembered something I have to do." *Like shove my head in the ground and surgically extract my wolf from my soul.* I managed to finish coming down the stairs and stopped in front of her. "You wanted to see me?"

If she was weirded out by my episode on the stairs, she didn't show it. "Yeah, you left this at the bar last night, and I just wanted to return it to you." She held out a white envelope, which I knew was filled with the cash I'd left her.

"Keep it," I said, lifting my palm. "I left it for you. For the drink."

"I can't accept this, it's too much." Shiloh took a step forward, and I got a fresh hit of citrus and spice.

"Well, now I know for next time." I took a step back, fighting every urge to lean in and inhale deeply. "I don't go out much, so I wasn't sure how much was appropriate to leave."

"Next time, huh?"

Maybe it was my imagination, but I swore the corner of her mouth ticked up when she said that. She came closer again, and every time her scent filled my nose, I had to hold back this surging *want* that overrode my system. I didn't just want to scent her, I was desperate to know if her skin felt as soft as it looked. Would she have that same citrus sweetness between her legs?

Holy fucking moon, I was in trouble.

"You don't have to wait until next time."

Oh no? So I can take you upstairs and taste every sweet inch of you right now?

My teeth ground hard in my jaw. I did *not* have

thoughts like this, especially about women I didn't even know.

"I'm here now so you don't have to learn such an expensive lesson," she continued saying, and I only distantly realized she was still talking about the money. "Please take this back, Orson. I insist."

"Keep it," I said roughly, pulling the reins on my lust to the best of my ability. "That was how much I chose to leave. So please accept it."

Shiloh's hand fell to her side, her face flushed with exasperation. "What's this really about, Orson?"

"Nothing. It's my appreciation for the drink and the exemplary service I received."

"Riley poured you *one* beer. We didn't even bring it to your table."

I shrugged. "It was a really good beer."

Her hand shot out toward me again. "You...are impossible. You know that?"

"What happened to your arm?" I growled.

Shiloh stared at the white bandage before drawing her arm back to tuck it against her body. "Nothing, just an accident with a broken glass. Happens all the time."

Her scent changed in that moment, the sweet citrus taking on a sour note. Fear. And my keen hearing picked up the change in her tone as well. She was lying. But why?

My wolf growled behind my sternum and, despite our earlier arguing, we were of the same mind right then. Someone hurt Shiloh, and she needed protecting.

"Anyway," she said dismissively. "If you're not going to let me return this, I'm just going to donate it."

"It's yours. Do what you like with it," I said.

"Fine." She turned to leave.

"Shiloh," I called out before being fully aware of doing so.

She faced me again and my mind blanked out. I didn't know what to tell her, if anything at all. Maybe I should ask her something instead? If she wanted to get dinner? Coffee? A drink? Was it stupid to ask a bar owner out for a drink?

Shiloh cocked her head, her face expectant while I mentally ran on a hamster wheel. My wolf was no help either. His brilliant idea was to march right over to her, run my nose along her neck and inhale her like a drug.

"Just be careful," was what I eventually blurted out.

She nodded slowly, and that was how I knew I'd said something extraordinarily stupid. "Sure thing. I'll do that."

Shiloh then turned and left the werewolf lodge, her addictive scent going with her.

CHAPTER 6
SHILOH

I was starting to dread work every evening. Once the last customer left and Sawyer came to pick up Riley, my gut would churn as I watched the door, waiting for that dragon shifter to come and collect his potion, which after three days, I hadn't even started on.

Running the bar was a full-time job and a half, even with an employee. Even on my days off, I ran around town on errands for my business. By the time I fell into bed every night, I was exhausted.

I used to love it. This business was my baby, my one true love. Throwing myself into work was the main way I'd gotten over Sawyer and how I realized I didn't need a partner to be happy. With Stout & Spirit doing so well, and being able to serve my community with this bar, I had been fulfilled.

Now it felt like a massive burden that I couldn't shake. Something that was in the way of the main objective: making this impossible potion for a shady dragon shifter so he wouldn't set the territory I loved on fire.

What could I do besides close the bar for a few months?

People would get concerned and ask why, and what could I tell them? Not to mention the income I would lose when I needed to purchase a whole slew of rare ingredients. And that didn't even solve the issue of somehow procuring the extinct ingredient, silver deadnettle.

To say I was stressed was the understatement of the year. As the days passed, the urge to break down and tell someone became overwhelming. Howling Death needed to know that an enemy was skulking around the territory.

But every time I came close, I pictured Vargmore on fire, my friends and neighbors running for their lives, running to save their children, family members, and belongings.

And I always came to the same conclusion—that it wasn't a risk I could afford to take.

So I pressed on in this hellish purgatory, choosing to shoulder the burden of this dragon's wrath myself.

"Hey, Shiloh?"

"Huh?"

I blinked and looked up to find Kaz waving a hand in front of my face, his brow knitted with concern.

"You just spaced out for a minute." He dropped to his haunches to become eye level with me. Apparently, I'd sat down on an empty keg at some point. Kaz's wings fanned out slightly, as if to shield me. "You okay, Shi?"

"Yeah!" I forced out a laugh, stretching my mouth into a smile. "You know how it is. Just running through the perpetual to-do list."

Kaz's face relaxed, and he reached out to pat a friendly hand on my knee. "You work too hard."

"Nothing I didn't sign up for." I stood up from the keg and took a quick peek inside the cold box. "We all set?"

"Uh, yeah." Kaz cleared his throat, rising to full height again. "You're all hooked up for tonight."

"Thanks! I can't wait to taste that bourbon stout, I know you've been barrel-aging it for years and—"

"Can I take you out to dinner?"

The question came out in a rush of syllables that I didn't fully process at first. When I opened my mouth to say, *Sorry, what?*, that was when it hit me, and no sound came out.

Kaz's wings were pulled in tight to his back, the dark red feathers stiff as he waited for a response. His face was carefully blank, but he wouldn't have asked me if he was hoping for a no, would he?

"Kaz..." I trailed off while my brain sputtered, trying to think of a rejection that would land softly in the midst of everything else toiling in my head. The poor guy had no idea he was asking me out at the worst possible time.

"Kaz, you're awesome, and we have a great working relationship, but—"

The angel raised his palms with a kind smile. "It's all good. I can take no for an answer."

My heart sank because while he was smiling in a *no-big-deal* kind of way, his wings had drooped.

"I promise it's nothing against you or the fact that we work together," I insisted. "I've just...got a lot going on, and I'm not dating at all right now."

"Sure, I get it." He started stacking kegs, moving them fluidly through the air like they weighed nothing. "But if you ever change your mind and want a night off, let me know." He glanced at me over his shoulder. "And it would be just dinner. No expectations other than that."

"I know. And thanks, Kaz."

I had zero doubts that Kaz was a perfect gentleman, but there was a roughness to him that was unique among angels, and that certainly had appeal. Like all of his winged brethren, he was gorgeous. But those tattoos and the physicality of his work certainly put him more, well, down-to-earth. And that said nothing of the fact that he was kind and respectful to everyone, without that air of superiority many angels seemed to have.

Kaz would make someone very lucky one day. But even without all of my drama going on, and despite how much I adored him, I could never see that person being me.

For some reason, Orson's cold eyes and scowling face popped into my head, and my heartbeat quickened at the thought of him.

"Well, I'll get out of your hair," he said, the mood turning awkward as we just stood around.

"Wait," I protested. "Why don't you stay and hang out for a bit while we open? The customers have been dying to meet the brewer who makes all their favorites." It wasn't a lie, but I also felt really bad about turning him down. "Plus, you never know. You might meet someone."

Kaz chuckled, shaking his head dismissively, but his wings lifted and flared out slightly. "Alright, I suppose I could hang out for a couple drinks."

"You'll have fun, I promise." I squeezed his forearm. "We always get a great crowd on Friday nights."

))))⟩⟩⟩●€((((((

FOUR HOURS LATER, Stout & Spirit had every seat filled and was standing room only. Laughter and conversation filled the space with a warm, uplifting energy. One good thing I could say about werewolves? They were happiest when brought together, and that showed in the smiles, the back-slapping and playful shoving, the dice games on the tables, and the beer constantly flowing.

Riley and I were constantly running back and forth—pouring, mixing, loading and emptying the dishwasher, but we were having a blast. I knew this crowd, and they had always been good to their bartenders. People brought empties when they ordered more drinks. They told jokes and stories while they waited. Everyone was in a good mood.

Kaz sat at one of the tables with long benches on either side and had invited an angel friend to hang out. I didn't know the guy, but he was your standard-issue angel, gorgeous with long brownish-blonde hair that belonged in a shampoo commercial. The two angels were hanging out in mixed company—males, females, humans, and were-wolves. One human woman couldn't keep her eyes off Kaz, and he seemed to return her interest, occasionally chatting with his friend or one of his beer fanboys, but most of his attention lingered on her.

Atta boy, Kaz, I thought, wiping down the bar for the millionth time.

A good chunk of Howling Death were here as well, and the group of massive leather clad werewolves formed their own little ecosystem at another table. I described them like a black hole to Riley, and she laughed in agreement.

They seemed dangerous to other patrons at first. People steered clear, not wanting to offend the alpha of the whole territory or one of the males he commanded. But after a few drinks, people got curious and then eventually drawn in, usually by Tryn, the friendliest and most outgoing of the pack. He'd find someone alone, or maybe a couple or small group, and draw them into the circle of howls and black leather, and those people would feel like they found their new best friends.

Throughout the night, I kept looking over at the biker wolf pack, scanning the familiar faces for one that was notably absent. One with the palest blue eyes that would be impossible to miss.

And every time, I forced my eyes away the moment I realized what I was doing. Why was I even looking for Orson? Why did I keep replaying our conversation at the lodge, especially when he said, "Now I know for next time"?

I wasn't actually *hoping* for a next time. Definitely not.

The other thing my brain was stuck on was when he told me to be careful. Ever since then, it had felt like a strange mix of paranoia and relief had settled over me. Paranoia that he might have seen the dragon shifter that night, maybe knew what happened. And relief for the exact same reasons. At least then I wouldn't be dealing with this alone. At least then a Howling Death member would be aware of the threat against the territory.

But who was I kidding? There was no way Orson could know. And if he did, why would he care about me? He only said that because he was an awkward poodle in wolf fur and didn't know what else to say.

The really annoying thing was, the more I tried to not think of him and focus on work, the more insistently he pressed on my mind. It felt like he was right behind me, following at every step. As the night went on, I even started to feel a sensation on my skin like he was running a touch along the back of my neck, caressing my hands and arms.

When the front door opened, bringing a new customer in along with the cool night air, I didn't have to look up from the drink I was making. I knew.

"There he is!" Tryn's jovial voice boomed over the din as

he greeted Orson with an aggressive handshake and slap on the back. "'Bout time you showed up. What are you drinking?"

I didn't hear Orson's reply over the noise in the bar and my pulse pounding in my chest and ears. I had to bring my palm to my heart and just stop for a moment. My heartbeat was fast but not in a frantic, racing way, just elevated and… excited? I was already in a good mood from the busy night, but my body seemed elated on a level that my brain couldn't understand. Sure, it was a busy night and I was active, but this was something else. Some kind of emotional response to…something.

"You alright, Shi?"

A broad body came into view, framed by a set of dark red wings. Kaz had his arms full of empty glasses and he was smiling, his face flushed with good cheer.

"Couldn't be better." I took the empties he put down and stuck them in the flats. "I should hire you as a busser."

Without looking, I somehow knew Orson was on his way up to the bar. It was like some invisible thread between us was being wound up, forcing the distance between us shorter and shorter.

Kaz laughed at my joke, taking no notice of the icy-eyed wolf coming up next to him. Orson rested an elbow at the bar and seemed content to wait. At least, I assumed he was content, considering he was looking at the angel like he wanted to turn him into an ice sculpture on the spot.

"What can I get you next, Kaz?" From all signs, the angel was tipsy and enjoying himself but nowhere near sloshed. He'd be fine to have another round or two.

Kaz reached across the bar and touched his fingertips to my arm, his eyes taking on that heated look I'd seen before. "Any chance you've rethought having dinner with me?"

The next thing I knew, the whole room went ice cold. And I knew exactly who it was coming from.

"Kaz—"

"*Don't.* Touch. Her."

Both of our heads whipped to face the snarling werewolf at the bar. Orson was holding his wolf back but losing the fight with each passing second. His teeth elongated while pale fur lightened his dark hair, and his ears migrated to points at the top of his head. Deep, rumbling growls rattled his heaving chest with every breath.

"Whoa." Kaz stepped back, his hands up defensively as his eyes darted between Orson and me. "I didn't know there was, uh—"

Orson turned with a growl, heading for the door. The entire bar had fallen silent at that point and stared as he stormed out.

I couldn't begin to explain what I did next. Couldn't make heads or tails of why my feet took me around the bar and chased after that werewolf.

The outside temperature felt the same as inside, that was how frozen over Orson made the bar feel.

Looking left, I saw Howling Death's fleet of motorcycles parked closely together under the porch light. Orson wasn't anywhere near them. Looking right, I saw the silhouette of a man pulling his shirt off as he walked away.

The moon wasn't full yet, but she would be in about a week, and it was a clear night. Orson's frame—the long arms, powerful shoulders, and tapered waist, were outlined in silver as he made for the treeline.

"Orson, wait!" I ran after him, still utterly clueless as to why. I was just along for the ride in my own skin, unable to fight this pull to the surly, loner wolf.

He ignored me and even picked up the pace. He was still more man than wolf, upright as he hurried away from me.

"Orson, stop! Please." I couldn't let him leave, that was the only thing I knew for sure. *Please don't leave me,* my heart seemed to cry out.

He finally stopped and spun around, silvery fur speckling the flat planes of his still-human chest. His breaths were still ragged and tinged with growls, abs flexing while every exhale of steam into the night air.

"Get away from me, Shiloh." His voice was warped from the shift. "Don't come any closer."

What the fuck? Those words had no right to hurt so much. I barely knew this guy, so why did my chest clamp up so painfully?

Some emotion must have come across in my face because Orson's tone softened. "I can't control my wolf right now, and I don't want him to hurt you. Please just stay back."

Something clicked right then, like a missing puzzle piece finding home in that perfect empty space. Without knowing *how* exactly, I knew what to do.

I reached toward him, palm out and low like I was offering a dog a sniff. "Let me touch your wolf."

"Shiloh, no." The man recoiled. "He's feral. He'll—"

The wolf came forward, cautious but curious.

Orson hadn't shifted. His wolf and I were meeting on another plane, energetically. My magic reached forward and the spirit of the animal inside Orson met my energy in the middle.

I gasped when I saw the wolf in my mind's eye. "Oh, you're so beautiful."

He looked like the moon in wolf form, silver with undertones of dark gray. Not quite white or cream or black anywhere. And, naturally, he had those same pale blue eyes as his human side.

I sensed a cold barrier around this wolf as well, a wall of isolation, or maybe protection?

His energetic form inched closer to me. It seemed he wanted to come right up and sniff me, check me out, but remained apprehensive.

"You're a gorgeous creature," I continued to praise him. "So strong and so fierce. But you wouldn't hurt anyone unprovoked, would you?"

The wolf lowered his head and growled, lips pulling back to show his teeth.

"Oh, you would?" My voice wavered with fear. This wolf wasn't the biggest one I'd seen, but I got the sense he was unpredictable. Feral, as Orson had said. "Who are you angry at? Kaz?"

The animal licked his lips, the growl from him long and continuous. *Anyone who would hurt you.*

It was more a feeling projected to me than words, a well of deep, protective instincts.

My heart lifted and soared, as if that was what I'd been waiting to hear. But I'd unpack that later. Right now, I had to talk this wolf off the ledge.

"Kaz won't hurt me, he's—"

Also anyone who would claim you. You're our *witch.*

Oh. Wow. Okay.

The elation in my chest soared even higher. I blinked away tears like I was on the verge of weeping with joy, but what the actual fuck?

"No one has claimed me. I belong to no one," I heard myself say. "And I'm safe, thanks to you."

Only that seemed to calm the wolf. The growling and teeth-baring stopped, and he came closer with a soft whine. I felt luxurious, dense fur under my palm, and then the soft lick of a canine tongue.

Before I could say anything else, Orson called him back and the energetic connection was broken with a flash of light.

I shielded my eyes and blinked, trying to see through the dark spots clouding my vision. But the man was gone, and I only saw a glint of silver fur through the trees beyond before that too disappeared.

CHAPTER 7

ORSON

Well, now I knew for a moon-damned fact that I would never show my face at Stout & Spirit again.

I could still keep an eye on Shiloh through my tree cameras though. It was the only comforting thought as I re-watched the footage from the past few nights. Yeah, all familiar faces coming in and out. None that seemed to strike fear in her. So why had I smelled it on her when she came to the lodge, and why did she lie about that bandage on her arm?

Maybe the better question was, why did I care so much?

Oh, look. There was me storming out of the bar on the camera feed because I could smell that angel's attraction to Shiloh and my wolf went batshit. I had to get away from everyone, especially him, in order to avoid a bloodbath.

The absolute last thing I expected was for her to follow me.

I wanted to bury myself alive while that whole thing went down. I was still open to the idea now, as a matter of fact. My wolf, on the other hand, was pleased as punch.

He strutted around underneath my skin, nose to the air with his coat fluffed out. He loved that she had bypassed me to reach him directly.

Shiloh had soothed my wolf, reassured him that he didn't need to murder anybody. Hell, she probably saved that angel's life. I didn't fully understand how she did it, but witches had all kinds of tricks. Whatever she did had worked. My wolf would have eaten out of her hand if she'd had a treat.

More than anything, my animal felt victorious that she had chased after us. In his eyes, she had *chosen* us, not that angel who had been making his interest clear right in front of her. She reached her hand out to him and said he was beautiful, strong, and fierce.

"It's not like that," I tried to tell my animal half. "She didn't choose us for shit. She just didn't want us to cause a scene."

But he was having none of it, spinning in circles and making happy little yips and barks. As misguided as he was, I could understand his elation. Nobody had chosen us before. Nobody wanted us, wanted *me*. Not when I was feral, or even before then. Not until Tryn talked me into joining Howling Death; and even now, I was sure Derric would trade me for another pack treasurer if he had the opportunity.

Pack life claimed to be all about community and taking care of your people, but I filled a role. That was it. If I wasn't so good at what I did, I could be replaced.

Nobody chose me just because I was me.

My wolf let out a low whine, his snout drooping and his ears falling back. He hated that I was raining on our parade, that I never let us be happy.

"'Cause that's when they get you." I stood from my desk

chair and stretched with a groan. "Just when you think everything's going great, they pull the rug out from under you."

Even I could recognize that I was spending too much time in front of the computer screen, thoughts spiraling around a drain, so I figured it'd be a good time for a run. All surveillance had been reviewed, financial reports run, and no one needed phones or computers repaired, so off I went.

Of course, who else but Tryn would I run into just as I was leaving?

"Hey, Orson," he called from one of the recliners in the loft outside our rooms, as if he was waiting for me to come out.

I grunted out, "Hey," as I hastily turned to lock my door.

"You left the bar pretty quickly last night. Everything good?"

"Peachy." I headed for the stairs without so much as a glance at him.

"Our wolves are always right, you know," he called out.

That gave me pause, my shoe hovering just over the middle landing. Looking up at the loft, I saw that Tryn hadn't looked at me either. His nose was in a book.

"What are you talking about?" I asked.

"Nothing in particular," he quipped, turning a page. "Just saying. Trust your wolf."

Tryn supposedly had some witch-like abilities himself, although I never put much stock in it. Others in the pack said he could see people's fate threads and that he sometimes could see the future.

My wolf's tail wagged at the acknowledgment, pleased that someone else believed him. I just shook my head and kept on going, crossing the open floorplan of the lodge as I headed out.

I'd left my motorcycle at the bar last night but didn't feel inclined to retrieve it yet. I just wanted to run Shiloh, and everything that happened that night, out of my system. I ran my four paws ragged that night after my wolf had essentially claimed her as our mate, and it still wasn't enough.

Shiloh was not for us. She was not ours, and I had to make my animal side see that.

With the full moon approaching, I'd have control over my wolf for maybe five more days at most. On that night, when the moon was as round and bright as she could be, the animal would take the wheel, and my human side had no choice but to strap in and go along for the ride.

Maybe I'd have Derric stick me in a kennel that night instead of going on the full moon run with the pack. I had no doubt exactly where my wolf would go once he was in control.

Unless I got her out of our system first.

I went around behind the lodge, away from the main road and any possible onlookers. Shifters and, for the most part, witches, didn't bat an eye at nudity, but Vargmore had a sizable human population too, and some of them were weird about it. Sawyer's mate still covered her eyes when males stripped down to shift because she had been raised as a human.

For me, it was the reverse. It took a while before I'd gotten used to wearing clothing and seeing others wear it all the time in their human skins.

After stripping down and tying my clothes and shoes into a tight bundle, I called my wolf forward and allowed the shift to take over. My eyesight dulled while my senses of smell and hearing dialed up way past human ability. The first thing I did was lift my snout to the air, hoping to catch notes of citrus and spice.

And just as quickly, I brought my head down and pressed my nose into the dirt. The scent of earth, grass, some of my packmates, and a raccoon, filled the space I had momentarily wanted to fill with Shiloh's scent.

That was all it was. A temporary lapse in judgment. Wolves were so scent-focused. She was merely the first pleasant smell my animal brain sought out.

I grabbed my clothing bundle in my jaws, then stuffed it into one of the cubby-hole shelves lining the back wall of the lodge. Someone, probably Derric, had built these shelves years ago for exactly this reason.

Once my clothes were secure, I was off, four silver paws flying over the forest floor.

I had no destination in mind, no scent trail to follow. But I ran like something was chasing me, like the image of Shiloh's face in my mind, lit up by moonlight, was something I could escape.

She stayed with me though, ever present as I ran. I came to a stop at a trickling stream, throwing my head back to let my wolf howl before continuing on my run.

He wanted to go to her, turn in the direction of Stout & Spirit to see what the pretty witch was up to. Maybe she would have a meal with us or rub our belly.

No, I ordered. *We will only protect her from afar.*

My wolf grunted and snuffled out his disagreement but didn't fight me for control. I should have known trying to appease him with the security cameras wouldn't have been enough. If I gave him an inch, when it came to Shiloh, he would take the whole damn road.

No more, I told my wolf, myself. *She doesn't want us. She doesn't even like us.*

She likes me, my animal huffed.

Yeah, too bad he and I were a package deal.

I spent the morning venturing deeper into the woods, looping around to the north side of the territory. Sawyer's cabin was around here somewhere, the one he built and lived in even when he was single. I envied him sometimes, that he could just get away from the lodge and the pack whenever he wanted to. Also that he had no problems socializing with others despite being a massive introvert as well. That was where he and I differed.

I brought my nose to the ground, seeing if I could pick up Sawyer's scent so I could steer clear of his personal territory. He probably wouldn't care if I was nearby but still, I didn't want to intrude if he and his mate were at home.

I walked leisurely as I scented the ground, muscles aching slightly from all the running. Out of nowhere, a scent trail grabbed my nose and pulled it like a magnet.

My tail started whapping back and forth. Happy high-pitched growls and barks left my throat. Citrus and spice filled my nose, my lungs, my brain.

Shiloh was nearby.

My wolf was practically fucking dancing, my front paws tapping an excited rhythm on the ground.

Moon be damned, was there no getting away?

Unable to help myself, I glued my nose to her trail and inhaled deeply. There was something else with her scent. Not the sour fear I'd smelled earlier, but something negative, along that vein. It was less pronounced, more of an undertone. Stress or frustration, maybe?

I tried to back away from the scent trail, but my wolf would not be deterred. He fought me hard, snapping his jaws and growling at what he saw as my short-sighted human consciousness.

Our witch is in distress. We must protect her.

She's fine, I reasoned. *Besides, another packmate is nearby. The enforcer will protect her.*

Shit, wrong thing to say. A growl rattled up through my throat and ribs. My wolf was *not* pleased at the idea of another male protecting our witch. That was our job, no one else's.

I took off running, following Shiloh's trail, and it might as well have been the full moon for all the control I had, which was precisely none. Only she had ever gotten this reaction out of him, driving the animal's instincts to override the man's.

Not even my years as a feral shifter had prompted my wolf to take so much control outside of a full moon.

When I came upon her less than a mile away, Shiloh was walking a barely-marked trail, one most often used by witches and humans. And fuck me, she looked adorable, which was not a thought I'd ever had about a woman in my life.

She wore a wide-brimmed hat to keep the sun out of her eyes, a light flannel shirt, jeans, and hiking boots. It was all practical and no fuss, but she looked every bit a modern hedge witch out in search of ingredients for her potions.

Actually, with the leather satchel at her hip and the ancient-looking book she was thumbing through, that seemed to be exactly what she was doing.

I could smell her frustration much more clearly now, and there was a deep furrow in her brow as she checked her book, then knelt to peer at a cluster of purple flowers next to the trail.

She didn't see us, and I was content to keep it that way. My wolf had other plans, however. He went straight up to her, tail wagging and tongue lolling out in a big ol' smile.

Sweet moon, bury me now please.

Shiloh was so surprised, her butt planted on the ground as my wolf bounded over. "Oh, hi!"

He wanted to lick her face, to get an inhale of that sweet scent up close, but hung back, giving her space. He sat like a good boy though, puffing his chest out like, *See? I am a well-behaved gentlewolf.*

Inside the wolf's skin, I was so taken aback, I forgot all about trying to regain control. My wolf never tried to put on a show of good behavior for anyone, and here he was, showing restraint for this witch that he believed to be ours.

Shiloh's shock appeared to wear off, and her stare was more curious than anything. "Are you in there, Orson?"

My wolf barked an affirmative. As for me, it felt like she was on my front porch and I was hiding behind a closed door.

"Looks like you're alright after the other night," Shiloh mused. Her eyes darted over my fur as if checking me out for injuries. My tail wagged harder at her show of concern.

"It's not a full moon yet, so you've got to be aware in there, right, Orson?" She cocked her head. "Or are you taking a nap or something while your wolf comes out to play? I don't know exactly how shifting works."

If she wanted to believe I was asleep inside my wolf fur, that was good with me. No way was I pulling my animal back. Even if I could, what would I say to her? Plus, I was naked. Ordinarily, that wouldn't matter, but for some reason, it didn't feel appropriate with her.

In any case, my wolf was far more confident with her. I was more liable to fuck something up if I opened my mouth, so I was content to sit back and let my animal side charm her.

In answer to her question, my wolf lowered to his belly

and crawled toward her a few paces before lowering his head to his paws.

Shiloh smiled in return, stretching out a tentative hand. "Is it okay if I pet you?"

I let out a low, rolling bark and my tail whipped back and forth over the ground. Shiloh's hand touching down between my ears was like receiving a kiss, the contact sending a wild thrill through me despite how hesitant and gentle it was.

"You're softer than I thought you would be." Her fingers curled, digging into the mane of fur around my neck before stroking down my back.

It was fucking heaven. My animal controlled the response but I was right there with him, lifting our head to butt against her palm, tongue darting out for not just a quick taste but some returned affection I never would have had the guts to give her in my human skin.

"You're sweeter than I thought you'd be too," Shiloh mused, a wry smile pulling at her lips. "Orson's a little bit prickly, isn't he?"

My wolf let out a soft howl in agreement.

Kiss-ass, I thought.

We inched closer to her, until our snout was practically in her lap. She smelled wonderful, juicy orange and the sharp bite of cinnamon in my nose. And oh sweet fucking moon, now she was petting me with both hands, giving long, luxurious scratches from my neck to my haunches. A long groan escaped the wolf's mouth as he flopped to the side and that noise was all me, not him.

I'd never had anyone touch me this much and had no idea what I was missing. Shiloh's hands running through my fur was pure pleasure, even though there wasn't anything remotely sexual about this.

Her touch, her scent, the warm sunlit ground, and her laughter at my wolf being an idiot. Just the combination of everything happening felt so good. So *right*.

Shiloh scratched at my chin, still chuckling. "Maybe you can help me, Orson's wolf."

Together, my animal and I snapped to attention. We rolled upright with a bark, alert and ears pricked, ready to provide for our pretty witch.

She smiled broadly at our response, then opened the book she'd been holding, turning it to us. "Do you recognize this plant? I need it to make a potion, but I don't recall ever seeing it."

One side of the page spread had an old, dried specimen of the plant itself, which didn't look like anything to me besides brown lumps. The other side had an illustration which did look familiar. I nudged the specimen with my nose, seeing if I could pick up a scent that might trigger a memory.

Instead, I got a nose full of dusty, ancient paper and proceeded to have a sneezing fit.

"Oh, I'm sorry!" Shiloh slapped a hand to her mouth but too late, she was already laughing her ass off. "Poor baby!"

After sneezing about a dozen times, I took another, more careful whiff of the page and got a familiar scent, faint though it was. I gave Shiloh a curious look, sitting on my haunches and cocking my head to the side. If I was right, this plant grew only on the highest peaks in Vargmore. It definitely wouldn't be growing along some trail down at this elevation. Not that I knew anything about witchcraft, but what kind of potion would call for such a rare, fickle plant?

Shiloh's expression turned serious, if even grave. "You know what this is?"

I gave a high-pitched bark and wagged my tail. At least, I was pretty sure.

"You know where it grows?"

My tail wagged harder, and I let out a soft howl at the sky.

"Can you take me there?"

I stopped my tail and pointed my nose at the ground. It would take days of treacherous hiking for a human to get there. No way in hell would I subject Shiloh to that.

But I could make the trip myself in probably a day.

"No?" Shiloh's face fell. "Please, Orson? I really need this. And I need a lot of it."

My wolf darted forward and licked her face before I could stop him, and then we were off.

We tore through the woods, a silver shadow on four legs heading north toward the mountain range. Behind me, Shiloh called after us to wait, but she would lose us soon.

We will provide for our mate, my wolf proclaimed. *And she will stay safe.*

I couldn't have fought him even if I tried. Just like the first time those protective instincts over Shiloh woke up, the animal drive blended into the human side. His will was my own.

Not even the feral shifter packs deep in Vargmore's forest went up to those peaks. The climb was brutal even on the clearest, warmest days. But for her, I'd do it without a second thought.

My mate was worth it.

CHAPTER 8

SHILOH

The moon's magic affected every living thing in Vargmore. Werewolves were the most obvious expression of magic, but even a blade of grass acted as a sponge, soaking up moonlight every night. Humans and witches were obviously affected too.

My family was said to be some of the first humans in Vargmore, here almost as long as the werewolves were. So we had a long, deep history with moon magic. It flowed through our veins just as potently as the blood that kept us alive.

Which was precisely why, on this full moon night, I was staring at my collection of sex toys with despair.

They were lined up on my coffee table like dead soldiers. Which they were, in the used up and out of juice sense. All of my electrical outlets were filled with chargers and batteries because somehow, none of my battery-operated-boyfriends had been able to make me come.

For the first time ever, literally *none* of my toys had been able to do their only job.

I fanned my face and paced my tiny studio apartment,

gulping down some water while repeating *what the fuck?* in my head. Being extra horny was expected on the full moon. Pretty much all sexually-reproducing females in their prime felt an extra boost of fertility during this time, whether you were a werewolf, human, witch, rabbit, or a praying mantis.

But this? Burning through the batteries on *all* of my vibrators and not getting an ounce of relief? This was bullshit.

In the words of some human rock band I saw on TV, *I can't get no satisfaction.*

At this point, it just felt like I was making myself more wound up and even hornier. I'd really just been edging myself for the last two hours, even though that wasn't what I was trying to do. I was hot and my skin was overly sensitive. Even my feet pacing over the floorboards felt like an erotic touch that wouldn't bring anything out of me.

I turned and looked at my bathroom, wondering if an icy shower would do the trick. It wasn't a pleasant idea, but I was getting desperate at this point.

My eyes then landed on the tied bundle of long stems with tiny, white-silvery flowers hanging upside down to dry next to the door. A bouquet of silver deadnettle, the main ingredient in Visakari's Kiss, one which I thought had gone extinct, had just shown up on my doorstep three days ago.

Even without the remnants of silvery-gray fur on the stems, it didn't take a genius to figure out how they had gotten there. And I couldn't stop wondering why.

I thought back to seeing Orson's wolf on the trail nearly a week ago, how friendly and dog-like he'd been. If Orson had been present and aware inside his animal, he didn't make that known. I imagined him inside his wolf like that night he came to Stout & Spirit alone, sitting back in a corner and not talking to anyone.

I'd known werewolves all my life and had never seen such a disconnect between the animal and human side. A surly, withdrawn man and a happy, outgoing wolf. The wolf side seemed to like me a lot, from that time on the trail and how he'd responded to my magic after storming out of the bar. What a shame that his human side seemed to hold a grudge against the very air around him.

My eyes darted back to the bathroom door and my next thought was trying the detachable shower head for some relief, which sent another full-body shudder through me.

"Damn it," I huffed, turning away to pace again.

Every time that bundle of flowers caught my eye, I didn't think of the beautiful, silvery gray wolf that flopped over for belly rubs. I tried, but my mind didn't go there. My mind was stuck on the man half of that incredible creature.

I thought back to when Orson growled, "Do. Not. Touch. Her," at Kaz, and nearly went to my bed to bend over on all fours, like the icy werewolf was right here, ready to mount me.

I wished he was.

Oh fucking moon, I wished he was.

In some distant corner of my mind, I knew my thought processes were being muddled by the big rock in the sky. My hormones were raging under the moon's magic, but I couldn't bring myself to care. Orson's rudeness, his complete lack of a filter, and misplaced possessiveness were the farthest things from my mind.

I couldn't stop thinking about his mouth and the white-hot intensity of those eyes. The height and breadth of him. All those carved slabs of muscle and how rough those hands must feel. I imagined his thighs straddling a motorcycle, or even better, splitting my legs apart as he drove into me.

Another shudder hit me, striking me with sensitivity from my clit to my mouth, parting my lips to let a moan escape.

I didn't know what it was about this full moon in particular, but I figured out in that moment that this aching need was for something specific. No toys would do the job because I needed a man to fuck me.

The answer was so simple, so obvious. I needed another person's touch, to be kissed breathless and penetrated by a man's body. I needed to feel the weight of him on top of me, feel the dizzying rhythm of his thrusts and his hands holding me down in the perfect position to take it all.

I was in bed before I knew it, thrashing around, legs scissoring for some relief as I twisted every which way in an attempt to get comfortable. In my mind, I saw Orson, kneeling on the mattress and gloriously naked as he stroked himself, every inch of him hard and tense as he waited for me.

Who knew why this moon made me yearn for a person instead of giving me run-of-the-mill horniness? Maybe this was nature's way of telling me I needed to get knocked up already, but whatever the cause, I could not let go of the mental image of Orson. Any attempt to replace him with another fantasy man was continuously booted. No one else would do. My body craved him and only him.

"Orson..." I moaned, slipping my hand underneath my shorts. I was soaked, and not just from the sweat pouring off me.

Toying with my clit did absolutely nothing though, not even when I imagined his hand in place of mine. The pleasure built and built but release remained just out of my reach.

"Fuck!" I growled up at the ceiling.

I was exhausted, wired, overstimulated, stressed as hell about this fucking dragon potion I had to make, with no way release steam...and lonely.

That last one hit me like a bucket of ice water, a realization as chilling as it was clear.

I had a full, busy life. I was a businesswoman and an active member of the community. But in my private life? It was just me.

There were lots of people I would consider my friends. People I could lean on and who I would be there for at a moment's notice. But obviously, no one I would invite over to fuck on the full moon. No one I wanted to share the burden of that dragon shifter's threats with.

Naturally, that last one was to protect others, but the former was all about me. After Sawyer, I didn't want to let anyone close enough to hurt me again. That was normal, right? Taking some time, *lots* of time, to myself after break-up. My normal brain saw the wisdom in taking a break from dating.

But right then, in my hormone-addled state, I was starting to think I'd rather die than spend the next ten minutes not being touched by a man.

A single long howl carried into my apartment from the cracked window, quickly followed by a chorus of howling. The sound dragged like fingertips over my skin, and a fresh rush of heat wracked my body.

Of course. I wasn't the only one affected by the moon's cycle. Howling Death and the other packs of Vargmore were running through the territory, their animals unrestrained by their human sides for this one night every lunar cycle.

Only one werewolf took up space in my mind, a silver beast with eyes like glaciers. Was Orson out there, howling with his kind and letting his wolf run the show? The feral beast that turned into a docile puppy with me. I couldn't imagine his wolf running seamlessly with a pack. I got the sense that he was an outsider, but not because he wanted to be.

The howling grew louder, and I wondered how late it was. This night felt years long,, but maybe the moon's rise had just crested, her power now waning as she descended across the sky and gave way to dawn. If that was the case, the werewolves would be heading back into town now, their minds growing clear as humanity returned to them.

My horny affliction was not lightening up though. If anything, the ache was becoming worse, almost painful enough to cry. I flipped to my stomach to scream my frustration into a pillow and promptly started grinding my pelvis into the mattress.

This was such fucking torture.

More howling came, this time sounding like it was just outside my window. As if the sound commanded me, my hips raised off the bed. My spine created a deep arch and my ass lifted higher as if in offering.

Presenting.

A scratching came to my door as I tried to make sense of what my body was doing, the tiny rational part of me wondering why I was responding in such a way to a wolf's howl. I was no wolf.

"Not a good time!" I called when the scratching came again. The sound felt like nails across my skin, teeth scraping my neck…

"Shiloh," called a rough, guttural voice through the door. "It's Orson. Let me in."

Yes! My body seemed to cry with relief, my back arching deeper. *Let him in. Inside. Deep, deep inside.*

"No, don't come in!" *Oh fuck yes, cum in...*

"Shiloh. Something's happening." Orson sounded more man than beast with each syllable, though his voice was still strained. "I don't think I can leave, even if I tried."

"You have to!" *Have to cum inside, so deep inside...* "I'm not...this isn't good!"

"I can smell you from a mile away," he said with a throaty groan.

"I'm sorry!"

"Don't be. Your scent is incredible." His voice softened but remained just as rough. "Like orange and cinnamon. I want it in my nose constantly."

Then come here and get a taste. The words were on the tip of my tongue, but I bit them back. "It's just the moon doing this to us," I said instead. "It'll pass. We just have to get through the night."

Only silence came from the other side of the door for so long, I thought Orson had left. His next words were so quiet that I could barely hear him through the muffled wood. "Or you could let me ease you."

Heat rushed through my body, lighting up all my sensitive points with an ache that begged for relief. I couldn't take another hour of this, let alone last until morning. I needed release, and on some primal, instinctual level, I knew he was the only one who could give it to me.

But we wouldn't have to go all the way, right? Despite my body responding to his howl with a face down, ass-up position, I did *not* want to be fucked by a werewolf I barely knew or even liked. I needed release. From him. That was all.

"Shiloh." I hated how erotic my name sounded on his

lips. "You're suffering. I can sense it. I don't know why this is happening but…I can take care of you. However you'd like."

His words seemed to soothe the aches wracking through me, and I grasped enough rational thought to roll over and cover myself with a sheet. I felt completely naked even though I still had clothes on.

"If I let you in…" I had to pause and bite my lip while my legs scissored with need. "Can you control yourself? I…I want us to talk and, I dunno, set some boundaries."

"I agree, we need to lay it out first." A muffled groan floated through the wood before he went on. "I'll control myself. You have my word. I just…you know, I just ran with the pack, and I left my clothes at the lodge…"

Sweet moon. There was a buck-ass naked werewolf on my doorstep.

And if the moon's magic was affecting him at all like it was me, he had to be sporting one hell of an erection.

Did I really want to do this? Let him into my home? Let him *ease me*, as he said?

Being rational was an effort in futility. No thought of Orson's personality came to mind. Only the richness of his voice, the width of his shoulders and contours of his arms. His lips and his eyes.

When it came to pure physical relief, I could certainly do worse.

"Shiloh?"

Fuck me, I almost wanted to keep quiet just to hear him say my name again.

"There's a blanket folded up on the armchair next to the door," I said. "You can cover up with that while we talk."

"Okay. So do I have your permission to come in?"

I waited, counting the seconds.

I only made it to eight before I heard, "Shiloh?"

A sigh escaped my lips as I threw my head back, and I tried not to think about how good it would feel if he moaned my name against my neck.

"Yes, Orson," I answered tightly. "You can come in."

CHAPTER 9

ORSON

Standing there on Shiloh's doorstep made me think of that old vampire myth about needing to be invited inside. It wasn't true, and I definitely wasn't a vampire, but I wondered if this kind of situation led to the perpetuation of that myth.

Two people on opposite sides of a divide, shoved reluctantly together by a strange, fickle magic.

When Shiloh called out, "Yes, Orson. You can come in," all thoughts of vampires left my mind. Instead, I pictured her underneath me, moaning *'Yes, Orson'* as I moved through her.

Just as quickly, I struck the image from my mind. This felt so wrong. My cock was heavy and aching, and I was about to enter her home on her invitation. But Shiloh and I both knew the truth—neither of us wanted this.

I wanted her, sure. But not like this. Not while she despised me and was only letting me in as a means to an end.

"Orson?"

My teeth sank into my lip, my canines still elongated

from my shift despite my wolf being oddly silent right now. I wanted to hear her say my name, over and over again while I wrung the pleasure out of her.

But this wasn't about me. I could smell Shiloh's pain through the heady bouquet of citrus and spice. She truly was suffering, and no one was around to help but me.

"I'm coming in." I gripped the doorknob in one hand while trying to cover as much of myself as possible with the other hand. I hated how sleazy this felt. Like I was some creep sneaking into an unsuspecting woman's home.

It was a wonder I didn't rip the doorknob from the wood from how hard my grip was. I swung the door open slowly, so as to not startle Shiloh, then slid in and closed it behind me as soon as there was enough room for my body. I spotted the blanket she had mentioned and grabbed it, wrapping it around my hips like a towel. The length of my erection pressed against my lower stomach, and while the blanket was soft, it was not the kind of friction I was craving. Still, I figured a bulge was better than a tent.

Only when everything was put away and in place did I allow myself to look at Shiloh. She was across the single-room apartment and felt worlds away. In her bed pressed against the opposite wall, she held a sheet to her chest. Sweat dotted her skin, and her face was flushed. Her breaths were ragged, and her delicious scent filled the room.

I needed to fucking breathe through my mouth. Inhaling much more of that scent would make me come into her blanket, and that was the last thing either of us wanted.

Neither of us said anything, so I figured I might as well start. "Thanks for letting me in."

She gave a slight nod and pulled the sheet higher on her

chest. I noticed she still had the bandage on her arm, and I had to hold my breath to stifle the growl that wanted to erupt from my chest.

Fuck, why did she have to be stuck with me to help her through this? Any other wolf would have been making her feel at ease. Charming and relaxing her before getting the job done.

"I've never been in this situation before." Shiloh winced as she made the confession. "It's never been this strong. I don't know why this moon is different."

"It'll pass, like you said." I meant to sound reassuring, but it came out dismissive and asshole-ish instead. "And I'll help you in any way I can."

Shiloh's eyes narrowed at me. "Have you done this before? Helped someone through her full moon...stuff."

It was impossible to lie, even though the truth felt like a betrayal for some reason. "Before I joined Howling Death, yes. A few years ago."

Those narrowed eyes widened. "When? Where?"

She was asking for information that few people had, information that I was not keen to give out freely. But right then, Shiloh could have asked me to cut off one paw so she could throw it into some witch's brew and I would have done so happily.

"I was feral before joining Howling Death," I said. "I lived with the wild packs and the traitor wolves deep in the woods. Sometimes, I would help unmated females through their fertile time at the full moon, just to ease them through it."

Shiloh cocked her head, and something like understanding flashed across her eyes. I didn't know what dots were connecting in her head, so I rushed on to explain myself.

"It wasn't exactly like this." I gestured between the two of us. "But similar enough, I guess."

I barely remembered hooking up with those females. Not because I was flooded with desire like now, but because they barely mattered. A female would find me, present, let me mount her, and then leave. Most of them I had never spoken a human word to. Even among the feral wolves, I was an outcast.

"How is this any different?" Shiloh asked, sitting up taller.

Their scents didn't drive me crazy like yours. They didn't have an attitude, weren't as smart or resourceful. None of them calmed my wolf like you did, rubbed his belly like you did. None of them had glossy black hair and freckles. They didn't have your laugh or smile. None of them were you.

While my head waxed poetic, what came out of my mouth was, "Well, none of them were witches." *Obviously, dumbass.*

Shiloh raked a hand back through her hair on a frustrated huff. I could sense the tension in her body. She wanted to wiggle and move but fought to hold herself together. Just like I was.

"Here's what's gonna happen," she said, dropping both hands over the sheet. "I have to...you know..."

"You need to come." The words left me before I could stop them, and I was already salivating. The scent of her in the air was delicious and potent, but I wanted more. I needed to taste it from the source.

Shiloh blushed deeper. "Yes, but without intercourse."

I had figured as much. She didn't strike me as someone who would fuck just to have an itch scratched. "That's fine with me. What would you like instead?"

"You can use your hands, I guess." Her gaze went down

to her lap, like she wanted to disappear and not be dealing with this, with *me*, at all. "And I'll take care of you in the same way."

As much as I loved the thought of her fist gliding up and down my cock with a gentle squeeze, there was no way in hell I'd have her do that. This situation already made her uncomfortable enough.

"Don't worry about me," I said. "Just let me take care of what you need."

She looked at me again, confused. "You're suffering just like I am. This doesn't have to be one-sided."

I scrambled for the words that wouldn't make me sound perverse, like the privilege of being in her home and being permitted to touch her at all weren't more than I deserved.

"Seeing you through this will be enough," I said.

Shiloh didn't look convinced. "I don't want to owe you anything."

"You won't. You have my word. I'll ease you, and then I'll leave. On my honor as a Howling Death wolf."

Shiloh's brows lifted in surprise. Invoking the name of my pack meant my promise was sacred, and I would be at risk for exile if I didn't fulfill my vow.

"You're sure?" she asked. "You'll just...help me take care of this problem and go?"

"If that's all you need from me, yes."

Shiloh's gaze slid away, and then she nodded as if convincing herself that this was what she had to do. "Okay then. Let's do this."

Neither of us moved, and I wanted to apologize. *Sorry for being so awkward that I can't put your mind at ease as well as your body. Sorry I'm not a male you actually want to do this with.*

A few seconds passed, and I cleared my throat. "Would you like to stay where you are? On the bed?"

She looked around as if just noticing where she was. "Oh. I can come to you, I guess—"

"No, that's alright." I took a step forward, one hand outstretched in an effort to halt her, the other holding tightly to the blanket around my waist. "Or just, wherever you're most comfortable."

Shiloh looked down and gave a sheepish little laugh, then patted the space on the bed beside her. "Maybe we'll both look back on this and laugh one day."

I wasn't laughing. I was starving. Approaching the bed slowly, a thought occurred to me as I sat down. "What if this happens again at the next full moon?"

Shiloh at least had the decency to not look disappointed. Her hooded eyes roved over my arms and torso. "We'll cross that bridge if we get to it."

"Okay."

Before the silence could get much longer or more awkward, Shiloh grabbed my jaw and planted a firm kiss on my mouth.

The shock settled in late. Only some time after our lips locked together in a hold, after my tongue darted inside for a taste and met her own, after I went to cradle her nape in my palm, after indulging myself in an exploration with light pulls and licks, did I remember where I was.

Shiloh was breathing harder when we parted. Her hands splayed over my shoulders while I had one hand on her waist and the other still holding the back of her neck.

"I didn't know kissing was allowed," I said, barely able to hear myself over the thundering of my heart.

Shiloh gave a little shrug, that slight smile returning. "Had to do something to get this started."

That reminder did nothing to quell the roaring in my blood. It didn't matter that she didn't want me or even like me, because I was here to provide for her, take care of her.

A satisfied growl rumbled up from deep within me, and it dawned on me then why I didn't notice my wolf. He and I were aligned perfectly in this, one and the same. *Satisfy our pretty witch. Ease her suffering.*

I kissed Shiloh again, using my grip on her nape to pull her in. Maybe I should have asked if more kissing was okay, but she gasped into my mouth and practically molded herself to me. She scrambled to push the sheet away, and my hand on her waist found its way to her bare legs.

She wore shorts and a tank top, and I kept my hands over her clothes in my awkward attempt to ease her, to encourage her to trust me. While I knew she wanted this over and done with, it didn't feel right to yank everything off and get straight to business. A cherished, respected mate was a satisfied one.

No, not mate. Partner, hook-up, whatever. I really needed to get that word mate out of my head.

Shiloh's legs spread wide of their own volition, and my light stroking of the outside of her thigh transitioned to the inside. We were still kissing, unhurried but passionate. Her hands explored me too, growing braver, although staying above my blanketed waist.

"Orson," Shiloh whimpered against my mouth. "Please...I can't take much longer."

I hooked a finger in the waistband of her shorts, holding in my howl when I realized how much she was squirming. "Can I take these off?"

Shiloh snapped her legs together and whipped off her shorts and underwear in one fluid movement. The next thing I knew, she had grabbed my wrist and pressed my hand directly between her legs. "Please, Orson," she begged.

Holy. Fucking. Moon.

She was so wet and burning hot. Her scent bloomed so strongly that I could practically taste her in the air. It was all I could do to not bring my mouth down to where my hand was.

"Fuck, Shiloh." I couldn't control the rough growl in my voice, nor the constant, pleased rumbling from my chest as she bucked against my hand.

"I'm so close," she panted. "You don't have to do much, I—ohh!"

I dragged my slick fingers to her clit and circled the firm little point, the place where she needed relief the most. The shift in her breaths and the increased volume of her moans told me I was on the right track. I wanted to keep watching her, to see the orgasm take over her body, but Shiloh grabbed the back of my head and kissed me again.

She moaned directly into my mouth, pulling and biting at my lips with a frenzied desperation. Fuck, how I wanted to bite her back. To leave a mark in her skin for everyone to see, so everyone would know the pretty witch was *mine*.

No, wait. No, she wasn't.

Shiloh's orgasm ripped through her on a full-body spasm and a scream that broke our kiss. I kept my hand firm between her legs, helping her ride out the tremors and rubbing every last ounce of pleasure out of her.

A sweat had broken out on her brow, and she could barely stay upright by the time it was over. Shiloh's hands planted behind her on the bed, her chest heaving as she stared at me with a serene, blissed-out expression.

"Thank you, Orson," she sighed.

I pulled my hand away from her and wanted to say,

You're welcome, or even, *My pleasure. Let's do that again some-time,* but I was choking.

Her orgasm had intensified her scent tenfold, and I was drowning in it. I was drunk on her orange-cinnamon flavor and like a damned junkie, I needed more.

But Shiloh was done. She'd gotten her release. If I didn't get the fuck out of here soon, I was afraid of taking things farther than we agreed on.

I said something, I didn't even know what, and started scooting away before I remembered the blanket around my hips. It started coming loose, and I paused to readjust it.

Shiloh came closer and I got a fresh, dizzying lungful of her scent again. She...what the fuck? She was kissing my cheek?

In my confusion, I turned to face her. And that was how I found our mouths locked together again.

Her tongue surged into my mouth. Short nails scraped my scalp and my upper back. She tasted so fucking good, and her waist fit so perfectly under my hands...wait, when did I get on top of her?

The next clear image I had was of Shiloh on her back, looking up at me. Her lips were swollen and red from all the kissing, her dark hair fanned out over sheets and exposed the slender curve of her neck.

Bite, my wolf roared. *Claim our mate.*

No. Absolutely the fuck not. Biting her was not what I came here to do. Actually, I kind of forgot what I'd come here to do. But it didn't matter because I was in bed with my mate and she was smiling up at me so sweetly...

Wait, no.

My brain was a mess of screaming, conflicting thoughts, like a dozen different people fighting to be heard.

The moon pulled me one way, my wolf another, and my human side was just trying to keep it all together.

What called to me the strongest, though, was Shiloh's scent. It drew me south, to the core of her. I needed to taste her properly and to please her again. One measly orgasm for her would not do.

Shiloh's tank top had ridden up over her stomach, so I kissed the edge of her ribcage and her bellybutton on my way down. Her skin was warm and so incredibly soft. Part of me wanted to stay, to linger and kiss more of her, but her scent called to me too damn strongly.

I held her thighs apart and wished I was stronger, that I could resist and leave, because some small part of me remembered that we weren't a couple, that nothing about this night would last. But I took my first taste of her and forgot all about giving a fuck about anything else.

She was the freshest, sweetest spring citrus I'd ever had on my tastebuds. Somewhere between an orange and peach. I took long laps of her while sealing my lips over her cunt to prevent any juice from escaping.

Shiloh was absolute heaven on my tongue, and I found myself closing my eyes and moaning against her body. At some point I realized she was rocking her hips, rolling up for more friction against my face. Maybe she was saying something too, but my hearing had gone fuzzy a while ago.

I did feel the scratching of her nails on my head and neck, urging me higher toward her clit. Once I felt satisfied with my fill of my mate's sweetness, I gave in to her demands.

I sucked her clit hood into a kiss, much like the many I'd given her mouth. Then I laved my tongue over the firm spot until she was thrashing against my face.

A fresh aroma of sweet citrus hit my senses, and I was

about to inch lower for another taste when I felt fingers in my hair forcibly yank me away.

"Stop," Shiloh panted. "It's too much."

Clarity hit me like a punch to the jaw. I backed away and saw her fully for the first time since I sat on the bed.

Now Shiloh was naked from the waist down, her top pushed up just under breasts, and her legs splayed wide. Her cunt was glossy, slick, and tender from what had just happened. There were even some red marks on her thighs.

Fuck, what *had* just happened? Her scent was clinging to me. I rubbed my face and sure enough, my mouth and chin had some wetness as well.

"Oh, shit." I got up and backed away from the bed, barely remembering to keep my blanket in place.

How could I fuck up so bad? I *told* her I could stay in control, gave her my word that I'd respect her boundaries, and I stomped all over them.

"Orson!" Shiloh started to get up, then remembered she was bottomless and hurriedly covered herself with a sheet.

"I'm sorry," I choked out. "Fuck, I'm so sorry."

"Orson, wait."

Shiloh might have started getting dressed, but I was already heading out the door. I couldn't stay a moment longer. She wasn't safe with me.

I dropped the blanket, shifted, and then took off running on all fours.

CHAPTER 10

SHILOH

"Well, this is some bullshit," I muttered under my breath, not for the first time that day. Or even that hour.

At the moment, I was peering into a cauldron. The fact that my potion ingredients weren't integrating correctly was indeed bullshit. The silver deadnettle turned out to be extremely sensitive to temperature and had broken down too quickly when I threw it in, despite following the potion instructions down to the letter.

It didn't help that every time I looked at that plant, it made me think of Orson, who had apparently harvested a whole bundle out of thin air for me. Who, after giving me two of the best orgasms of my life, jolted out of my bed like I'd horrified him and then ran out of my apartment like he was moments away from turning into a pumpkin.

And I'd thought Sawyer dumping me was traumatic.

It had been nearly a week since Orson left on that full moon night. The more I thought about it, the more my feelings seemed to get tangled up and confused. Parts of the night were hazy to me, which I could attribute to the moon's magic and the strength of those orgasms making me lose my mind.

But I remembered enjoying it. A lot. And in ways that had nothing to do with the release of suffering. Orson had kept his distance until he was sure I wanted to proceed. He didn't even make the first move. I had to kiss him first, and *holy shit,* nobody had ever kissed me like that. I expected him to be stilted and awkward, but his mouth fit mine like we had been made for each other.

And as I thought back to how he had touched me and tasted me, it seemed he was more in tune with my body than anyone else I had ever been with. I had been moments away from saying 'fuck the rules, get inside me now'.

But that was when he left in a big damn hurry, looking horrified and muttering about how sorry he was.

If that wasn't enough to make me swear off all men, especially werewolves, nothing was.

I went back to stirring my potion, trying to swirl all thoughts of Orson out of my brain. But try as I might, the bastard stuck, and not for any good reason.

It was damn hurtful how he left.

What I couldn't shake was not how thoroughly he pleased me, but how much it hurt me that he had left. It gave me such fucking whiplash. He'd been there when I'd needed him and was completely selfless the entire time. That blanket around his waist never came off once. And then it was like someone did a sudden personality transplant on him.

Or maybe it was the kindness and selflessness that was fake, and the rude, brusque asshole was the real Orson. Yeah, that made more sense. It was in line with just about every other interaction I'd had with him.

To add insult to injury, he hadn't come to the bar once since that night.

My usual Howling Death regulars came to Stout & Spirit, but Orson was never among them. I had walked my usual trail through the woods, where I'd rubbed his wolf's belly, and he was never around. In doing all my usual errands around town, I never caught a glimpse of him.

Naturally, that made me feel even shittier about what happened.

I couldn't dwell on it though, because the safety of the territory rested on my shoulders, and the clock was ticking.

Every night the dragon shifter hadn't returned, I had breathed a small sigh of relief. At the same time, I knew the reprieve wouldn't last forever. Stout & Spirit was closed tonight, and it was my first opportunity to make a test batch of his potion on the stove.

It was not going well, and when my front door swung open with a bang, my dread became a cement brick in my stomach.

"Come out, witch. I know you're here," he called.

My hands were already shaking so hard, I had to focus to turn the stove off. The mark, which I continued to keep bandaged because it *never* healed, burned like a hot brand was being pressed to my arm.

The dragon waited for me in the main dining area, drumming long black claws on the bartop as I came out from the back room.

"Well?" he huffed, wisps of smoke escaping his flared nostrils. "Where's my potion?"

"I—I was able to find all the ingredients, but—"

"But what?" he snarled. "What's the fucking hold up?"

"I need more time." My hands wrung together in front of me, and I wondered if there was any way out of this alive for me. "Please understand that no one has made Visakari's Kiss for hundreds of years."

"So what? You witches can live as long as we do."

"It's just that not all steps were recorded accurately in the grimoire, or they've been lost to time. I need to test the ratios of ingredients, find the optimal temperature, the best duration of the boil—ahh!"

The dragon only had to curl a few clawed, scaled fingers to make the pain in my arm unbearable. I clutched the limb to my chest, curling into myself while tears stung my eyes and only whimpers escaped my lips.

"Do you think you can play me, witch?" he asked coldly.

"I'm not, I swear!" I cried. "Please, stop!"

He didn't stop. My arm burned and pulsed, the pain shooting up to my chest and down into my stomach. I wondered if it would make my heart stop. Anything to make it stop.

Just when it felt like I was about to knock on death's door, the pain lifted.

I gasped for breath, my vision dotted with all kinds of dark colors. My stomach roiled, ready to empty itself from all the conflicting sensations.

"You have until the end of the month," the dragon said coolly, turning to leave.

"Please, you don't understand," I gasped. "You don't know what you're asking. It's impossible to do in that time. If I could do it, I promise you I would, but this solution is ancient and extremely dangerous. I'm doing everything I can, please don't hurt anyone..."

I was babbling, desperate. On some level, I knew my pleas were falling on deaf ears, but if there was even a sliver of hope that this psychopath would listen to reason and give me the tiniest of breaks, I would try. For the lives of everyone in Vargmore, I would try.

"The end of the month, witch," the dragon repeated, not losing a single stride on his way out the door. "Or your precious territory becomes rubble and ashes." He paused in the doorway and flashed me a toothy smile over his shoulder.

"Which would make it a perfect environment for a new clan of dragons, wouldn't you agree?"

CHAPTER 11

ORSON

"Not in the mood, Tryn," I called when the knocking came to my door for the third time that day.

A dry chuckle floated through the wood. "Good thing I'm not him."

Oh shit. I stood abruptly from my desk, pushing my rolling chair back. It hit the opposite wall as I went for the door and jerked it open. "Sorry, Alpha. I didn't realize it was you."

"Clearly." Derric flashed me a smile, the scars on his temples blending with the lines at the corners of his eyes. "What are you up to, Orson?"

"Just, ah..." I gestured vaguely at my monitors. "You know, keeping an eye on things."

"You know, I admire your dedication to your job in the pack," he said. "But you don't have to work *all* the time."

"Well, I—"

"No vampires have been sighted, so Thorne is apparently holding up his end of the deal." The alpha's lip curls at the mention of Blood 'til Dawn's president. "And our finances appear to be in great shape, thanks to you."

"Thank you, Alpha."

He nodded and leaned against my door jamb, with no intention of going anywhere. "So take a break and come out with me."

"Out?" I parroted.

"It's the fall equinox," he said. "The humans are having their equinox feast tonight. Come with me."

I blinked. "Why are you going to a human holiday feast?"

"Because the humans of Vargmore are still my people." A flash of regret crossed his face. "I need to make amends for how I regarded them before. So I'm spending more time with them and contributing to their feasts. I want them to know I'm here for them just as much as our own kind."

"That's noble of you, Alpha. I'd love to come, but I have a lot of—"

"Don't feed me excuses, Orson," he said with an edge of growl to his voice. "Like I said, the territory is secure. Our finances are good. Shit, everyone's got a working phone. What could possibly be so urgent?" When I didn't answer immediately, he smacked a hand against my stomach. "Great, meet us downstairs in two hours. Be ready to eat."

"Us?" My mind was still reeling over how I got roped into a social event with humans.

"Sawyer and Fallon are coming too, along with their mates." Derric flashed me a toothy smile as he headed off. "Don't worry. You'll be among friends."

))))))))))((((((

THE HUMAN LODGE was a single-story building in the northeastern part of Vargmore. From what little I understood about human culture, they didn't form packs like wolves did. Many humans lived independently, like Shiloh, or with a partner and any children they had. Their "packs" were more like small family units consisting of parents and children, sometimes including grandparents or aunts and uncles.

For this reason, no one lived at the human lodge. It was more of a meeting place or event center for their species. Conversely, all the unmated werewolves of Howling Death also lived at our lodge. The one exception to that I'd seen had been Sawyer, who built a cabin for himself and lived there full-time even before he found his mate.

Generally speaking, it just made sense to our kind that pack stayed together. As antisocial as I was, being a lone wolf wasn't in my wiring.

I wonder if Shiloh gets lonely, living and running a business by herself.

I pushed the thought away just as quickly as it had come. Shiloh's state of mind was not for me to know. I had no right to it, no right to any of her.

Not checking the tree camera feed for the past week was one hell of an exercise in self-restraint, one that my wolf threw multiple howling tantrums over. But that was the exact reason I had to stop. Protecting and pleasing Shiloh had become an obsession, one that was exacerbated by the full moon. If I saw that building, the Stout & Spirit bar with her little studio apartment on the top floor, I'd pour over the footage for hours just for a glimpse of the pretty witch. The woman my twisted mind kept referring to as my mate.

I had no mate. Fate would never be so cruel to a female, whether human, witch, or werewolf, to saddle them with me for all eternity. Shiloh especially deserved better. After I lost control and stormed past her clearly-laid boundaries that night, the very least she deserved was to never see me again.

After pulling my motorcycle up to the front of the human lodge, I went to help Derric unload his cargo for the feast. The smell of roasted seasoned lamb helped to combat the olfactory memory of citrus and spice.

Fallon, who was no longer an official Howling Death member, went up to the front door first, alongside his mate, Aria, who he'd met in his travels to the human world. She had believed herself to be human all her life, until his mating bite awoke the latent wolf within her. Sawyer's mate, Riley, was the same, except that she had been kidnapped from the human world by vampires.

The two mated females clearly still had strong ties to their human sides, which must have been why they wanted to celebrate the human holiday.

The heavy door swung open, and a cheerful, white-haired man enthusiastically invited us in. Derric and I followed behind the mated couples. I nodded a greeting at the human, who smiled so hard that his eyes were squinting.

"Happy Equinox, dear friends! We're so happy to have you join us!"

"Happy Equinox, Bodhi." Derric shook the man's hand. "I brought a crown roast. I hope it's to your liking."

The human, Bodhi, gasped. "Alpha Derric, you are too kind."

"Just Derric, please." The alpha smiled.

"Sweet moon, thank you for this. Here, we'll put it in the center of the table. Does it need to be warmed up?"

The two of them went off and another human showed me where to put the dinner rolls and wine I carried in. I remembered to say thank you and even tried my shot at a couple of smiles. Derric never told me explicitly, but I knew my behavior was expected to be polite. Courteous. Thank you was important. So was please. I should not take anything unless offered, and I could not start eating until the hosts said we could begin.

All the rules ran through my head. If Tryn were here, I knew his eyes would be burning holes into me.

Unsure how to occupy myself, I stood at the edge of the great room. Much like our own lodge, it was a single open space. Long rows of tables and benches filled the space, with a fire roaring in a stone hearth against a far wall and a large chandelier of deer antlers hung from the ceiling.

It was every bit a hunter's lodge. Warm and inviting, with people conversing over drinks and appetizers before the main meal.

And it all just made me want to run back to my room. Or maybe run in the woods in my wolf's fur.

"Orson!" Sawyer waved at me from one of the smaller tables where he, Fallon, their mates, and a couple of humans gathered. "Come sit. Have a drink."

"Yeah, no need to stand around like a ditched prom date." Fallon scooted closer to his mate and gestured at the empty space he left.

"I don't know what that means," I muttered as I dropped into the seat.

"Neither do I." Sawyer looked at his mate expectantly and she nodded.

"It's a human world thing," Riley confirmed with a pat to his arm.

Fallon's mate, Aria, leaned across the table to the human couple, a man and woman who looked to be in their twenties. The woman kept touching her belly, and she looked to be in the early stages of pregnancy.

"So you were telling us how humans are related to witches?" Aria implored them. "Go on, it's so fascinating to me."

"Right, so we're both the second generation in our families to live in Vargmore." The woman gestured to herself and her mate. No, wait, husband was the human term. "After three generations, enough moon magic accumulates in the bloodline that the next generation is born with magical abilities." The couple beamed at each other, linking their hands over the woman's belly. "Our daughter will be the first witch of our family."

"That's amazing," Aria gushed. "You must be ecstatic!"

"Well, it's still a bit early, so we're being cautious." The man gazed adoringly at his mate— no, wife. "But the pregnancy is strong and healthy so far. We're very optimistic."

"Congratulations to you both." Fallon raised his glass to them.

"If you don't mind me asking," Riley leaned across Sawyer to speak to the humans, "how did your ancestors end up in Vargmore? They must have come from the human world, right?"

The couple exchanged a look and chuckled. "Every human in Vargmore has a different story," the woman said wryly. "My father said he was following the railroad west, looking for work. One night, he had too much to drink, slipped, and rolled down an embankment. When he stopped rolling, he was somewhere completely different, and a huge wolf was growling in his face."

Sawyer laughed and gestured to the werewolves at the table. "That was probably one of our fathers."

"My uncle, maybe," Fallon said. "He didn't like humans."

I knew for a fact it wasn't my father. But I chose to keep that to myself.

"My mom was living in Ireland." The human man rubbed his wife's upper back. "Lots of people believed in the fae folk back then, all kinds of magical tricksters, monsters, and bogeymen, you know. They had these ancient ritual sites, giant stone circles that were said to be portals to the fairy realms. Well, my grandma was a rebel for her time. So she and her friends decided to visit one of the stone circles on the night of a full moon."

"That's not a recipe for hijinks at all." Sawyer chuckled.

"So they go out there. They're drinking whiskey and smoking cigars they stole from their fathers. Mom thought she must have passed out. The next thing she knew, she woke up and it was daylight." The human cast a conspiring glance across the table. "And you can probably guess what happened next."

Aria's eyes flashed. "A growling wolf in her face?"

"A whole pack of 'em!"

The table burst into laughter and declarations like, "Oh shit!"

"I'm just glad we can all sit at a table and eat together now." Riley clasped her hand in Sawyer's, whose eyes never left his mate's face.

"Times have changed for the better," he agreed with a low murmur.

When he brought her hand up to his lips to kiss the back of her palm, that was when my dumb mouth decided to open itself. "Fuck, Sawyer. Where'd you get that?"

I hadn't noticed before that Sawyer had a long black mark running down the back of his hand, from the knuckle of his middle finger to his wrist. The skin was raised and cracked like the bark of a burnt tree.

The other wolf shot me a casual smile despite the whole table looking concerned. "Ah, this is nothing," he said. "Just burnt myself on the barbecue. It looks worse than it is."

"Might want to clean your barbecue," Fallon said, his eyes rapt on Sawyer's mark. Looks like you got a bunch of soot embedded in that burn."

"It's really no big deal." Sawyer's voice went lower, serious and cold as he met Fallon's stare. "I can handle a little burn."

"I hope you can."

The two of them were speaking in some coded language. Everyone's eyes except Riley's bounced between the two wolves like spectators at a ping-pong match. Sawyer's mate just hugged both arms around his bicep, leaning her head on his shoulder. A show of support, if even protection.

A pair of doors burst open right then, and a line of people emerged from the kitchen, all carrying platters of food. Bodhi, the man who greeted us at the door, led the procession carrying a massive carved turkey. Derric followed right behind him with the crown roast. A human woman followed behind him with a honey-glazed ham.

"Vargmore friends, I hope you're all ready to eat!" Bodhi laughed jovially as he set the turkey down at the main table.

Once the main dishes were set, more people streamed

out of the kitchen with sides. There were casseroles, salads, root vegetables, and every type of grain dish you could imagine.

Bodhi bustled around the smaller tables as the dishes were set out, encouraging people to get started. "Please, don't wait for us. Help yourselves and find a seat. There's plenty enough for everyone!"

I stood up when our small table got moving, everyone encouraging the pregnant human woman to fill her plate first. It was only dawning on me then how important this holiday was to the humans. The main table, stretching nearly as long as the entire room, was filled with candles and matching table settings for each person. And people were still bringing out dishes.

Something citrusy with a hint of spice hit my nose, and I stifled a groan. Whoever cooked something with the exact same scent profile I'd been trying to avoid was fucking cruel. My wolf whined under my skin. He missed that scent so damn much.

I took a seat at the big table next to Sawyer, who was engaged in conversation with Riley on his other side. The benches filled up quickly as the kitchen volunteers finished up behind the double doors and came to eat. I was mid-swallow on a beer that I promptly choked on when the last of the kitchen staff came to the table and that incredible scent hit me so hard, I could have been taking a bite out of the fruit itself.

No, it can't be.

I didn't want to look but the pull of her was so strong, my resistance was laughable.

Shiloh's eyes darted away the moment they met mine, her face carefully blank as she found a seat that was thankfully not in my field of vision.

Fucking moon, why is she here?

The answer was obvious in hindsight. The witches of Vargmore were closely tied to the human community. Of the non-shifters at this feast, the split was probably fifty-fifty human and witch. A better question was, why the fuck did it not occur to me that she *would* be here?

While my head was reeling, my wolf was overjoyed. He'd been sullen and quiet for a full day, and like a magic pill, he was spinning in circles, tail going nuts, and pawing at me to go say hello to Shiloh.

In the span of a moment, none of the food seemed appetizing. Nothing would satisfy my tastebuds except the one thing I couldn't have—the witch I'd thoroughly fucked things up with.

I looked down the length of the table to my fellow were-wolves. Everyone was digging in, talking animatedly to their table neighbors, and in no rush to leave. How bad would it be if I just got up and went outside? And just happened to never come back in?

Well, I'd come with the alpha, who was an honored guest by the looks of it. Derric was seated next to the human leader at the head of the table. So chances were good my leaving abruptly would cast poorly on him. Damn it.

I took another swig of beer, keeping the glass near my nose in hopes of giving myself a different scent to latch onto. It was a poor substitute for the scent I really wanted, but it would have to do.

Don't look at her. Don't scent her. And definitely don't speak to her, I told myself.

I would endure. I would get through it.

Somehow I always did.

CHAPTER 12

SHILOH

Of all the places I thought Orson might pop up, a human equinox feast was the last one I expected.

A handful of werewolves were in attendance, which was a surprise. Derric seemed intent on being more present in the human community though, so bringing a main course and some of his packmates was a thoughtful gesture.

All throughout the feast, I kept focused on my plate and conversed with the people directly across and next to me. There was absolutely no way I would look down the length of the table to the icy-eyed wolf. No way in all the moon's glory. Sawyer and Riley were right next to him and I'd had yet to say hello, which felt rude. I'd have to find my way to them, as long as Orson wasn't around.

The longer I sat, eating and talking, the more my surroundings faded out of focus, despite my grasping to hold onto them. The anger and hurt I'd been trying to ignore took center stage.

I wished more than anything that those feelings would just go away, but it felt like I'd been snagged on a fishing hook. The more I fought, the deeper the barb embedded itself. I wanted answers, some closure at least. Did he really find me so unattractive? Was there something about me that was just repulsive to werewolves?

Even more, I resented that I had such questions at all, that I was an emotional barnacle on a guy that clearly didn't give a shit. Why should I care? Orson was rude and callous during the best of times. Why was I getting so worked up just eating at the same table as him? He clearly wasn't affected.

On and on the cycle went. Anger at him. Anger at myself. Resenting him. Resenting my own stupid feelings. All the while trying to smile and look cheerful to everyone else.

When it came time to clear everyone's plates, I could not get up fast enough. I wasn't even on washing duty this year, but I grabbed a bussing tub and proceeded to collect everyone's dishes from my area of the table just so I could disappear into the kitchen for some peace.

In the precious seconds I had alone, I sighed out an exhausted breath. I had barely gotten any sleep last night due to making more test batches of the dragon's potion. And now I was getting low on silver deadnettle, which posed another issue. I had no idea where Orson had sourced it from.

My alone time came to an abrupt end when Theda, a fellow witch, and Haley, a human woman, came through the double doors with their own bussing tubs full of dishes.

"How are they feeling about dessert out there?" I asked, making myself busy with sorting dishes in the sink.

"Most of 'em are saying no, they're too full." Haley set her collection of dishes down next to mine.

"Those werewolves can eat a lot," Theda smirked.

"Did you see the one with those stunning eyes?" Haley leaned against the counter. "I wouldn't mind giving him something to eat."

Neither of them noticed me freezing up as they laughed.

"I couldn't stop staring at the alpha," Theda sucked her lower lip between her teeth. "I just wanted to touch his hair. And those scars! You know they tell a story."

I cleared my throat loudly. "Let's get some tea and coffee ready, since almost everyone is skipping dessert."

"I'm on it!" Theda headed for the cellar.

"Get some ginger root for the tea," I yelled after her, then to Haley, "How about you get some plates together that people can take home with them?"

She waited for a beat before pushing off the counter. "Sure thing, boss."

My shoulder slumped. I had to remember she was just another volunteer, not the one in charge here. "Sorry. It's hard for me to snap out of work mode sometimes."

"All good, Shiloh." She smiled before digging out paper plates and food wrap cloths from a lower cabinet.

Barely a minute passed before the kitchen doors swung open violently. Three large werewolf bodies crashed through, and I'd have given anything to make myself invisible right then. Derric had an arm around Sawyer and Orson's necks, their heads practically in his armpits from the playful headlock. Sawyer grinned sheepishly and waved a greeting as he was dragged in by his president. Orson was stone-faced, his arctic eyes avoiding me. He too looked like he wanted to disappear.

At least we had that in common.

"Ladies, let us help you on cleanup duty." Derric released his packmates and gave them a light shove forward. "It's the least we can do after all your hospitality."

Haley and Theda were dumbstruck at the sight of the highest ranking alpha in Vargmore standing in the kitchen, so it looked like it was up to me to answer him.

"Nonsense, Alpha." I waved my hand in a shooing motion at the wolves. "You're our honored guests. Please, go back to the table and relax. We'll bring out coffee and tea soon."

"Then let us help you serve." Derric tossed a smile at Theda, who only managed a squeak of shock. "It'll mean less trips for the three of you. Besides, you've been working all day on this feast."

"About time for all of you to relax," Sawyer chimed in.

"See?" Derric slapped him hard on the back. "We want to help."

Well, at least two of them did. Orson looked like he wanted to run out with his tail between his legs.

"We will finish faster with extra hands," Haley said timidly. She stared directly at Orson, even though his gaze remained on nothing.

That alone made me want to double down on refusing, even shoo away the wolves with a broom if I had to.

"We have a...procedure," I said tightly. "Everything has to be left a certain way for the next kitchen shift. It would take longer to teach someone new."

"It's just for one night, Shiloh," Theda argued. "We don't have to train them on the whole process."

If I didn't need to look polite in front of three werewolves, I would have openly glared at her. *Et tu, Theda?*

Derric raised his hands. "We just want to help. If we'll be in the way, no worries. We'll stay out of your hair."

"Fine," I said, snappier than I intended. "Stay and help. Theda, do you have that tea and ginger root?"

The giddy smile wiped quickly from her mouth as she returned to all-business. "Um, yes, Shiloh."

"Good, let's start brewing. Haley, you want to show these guys the coffee maker?"

"Sure, this way!" She swung her hips as she walked, and it was a fight to not groan my disapproval.

"Someone should probably get a headcount of the table and see who wants what," I said instead.

"I'll go." Orson whipped around and left the kitchen so fast that the door had swung closed by the time everyone looked.

For some reason, his speedy exit annoyed me so much, I couldn't even take pleasure in Haley's disappointed expression. And still I knew, the moment he came back, I'd feel the same way about him being nearby. I didn't want him close, but that didn't mean I wanted to see him leave again.

Fuck Orson, and fuck the moon for making me want him.

Naturally, that was when a memory of Griselda's, one of the elder witches who raised me, voice popped into my head. *Moon magic is a clarifier. It purifies, distilling everything down to its true intent. And its light shines on what is already deep inside you.*

"Bullshit," I muttered as I set out cups and saucers for serving. I never wanted to sleep with Orson before that full moon night. And despite what my hormones were telling me, my desire had nothing to do with him in particular. He was just conveniently nearby. Then up and left like a jerk, which was why I was so annoyed.

He'd been an annoying jerk before then too. His wolf was okay, I'd give him that.

I didn't look up when the kitchen doors opened again.

Still, Orson's low voice touched my ear like a caress when he reported the number of requests for coffee and tea.

We got everything brewed, and the werewolves were surprisingly efficient, carrying trays packed with tea cups and coffee mugs filled to the brim, along with small pitchers of cream, sugar bowls, honey sticks, and stirring spoons. I was grateful to get swept up in the hustle and bustle, any excuse to not stew over Orson.

Once that rush was over, I found myself alone in the cool, basement cellar below the kitchen. Everyone had been served, so the girls and our werewolf helpers had resettled at the table with their drinks to wind down. My stomach wasn't feeling caffeine, so I opted to brew myself some herbs.

I grabbed what I needed and headed back up, frowning at the sound of water running and the gentle clatter of plates stacking together. At the cellar doorway, I saw a man standing over one of the deep sinks, spraying water over a pile of dirty dishes.

"What are you doing?" I asked before my brain caught up to what my eyes saw—the height, the wide set of shoulders, the dark hair cut short and then tightly faded as it went higher up his skull. The strong legs and...yeah, the ass. That ass was not one to be ignored.

"Washing dishes. What does it look like?" Orson answered without looking back at me.

I set my collection of herbs down on the island counter with a huff. "Don't worry about those. I'll take care of them."

"Just rinsing them off before the food sticks." He pulled down the detachable faucet head and clicked on the spray setting, waving it back and forth over the plates in the deep sink.

"You don't have to do that," I said with more force in my voice. "It's not your job."

"Not yours either. They said you weren't on washing duty this year."

"Well, I've been volunteering for years. I know how things are done."

"Right. You have a procedure." He released the nozzle to move the rinsed dishes into the next sink basin.

"We do. And it's not the way you're doing it."

"Then show me how." Orson lifted his head and turned, hitting me with that frosty gaze. "I warn you, though," he added before I could retort. "I'm a slow learner."

"That's not true," I blurted out before slamming my lips tight. Orson was highly intelligent from what I gathered, but I was not about to flatter his ego.

One large shoulder rolled in a lazy shrug while the hint of a smile played on his lips. "Maybe not when it comes to washing dishes. But I am about other things."

"Like manners." I crossed my arms, making my stance challenging. It was just me and him in the kitchen, so fuck it. Why not confront him?

Orson dipped his head. Not in a full nod but in a way of acknowledging what I said. "I'm not good with people. I'm trying, but I don't always remember the rules for every situation."

I loosened my arms just a little. That admission paired with what he'd said about growing up feral made sense, but I wasn't about to let him off the hook yet.

"Why did you leave like that?"

His head lifted but he still didn't meet my eyes. "Like what?"

Fucking moon, was he really going to make me say it? "Like you were...disgusted by me."

That icy gaze snapped to mine faster than a predator locking onto the scent of prey. "I was never disgusted by you." A growl rumbled up from his throat. "Not in the slightest."

"You backed away from me like you were horrified."

"I was," he said. "At myself."

"Yourself?" I shook my head. "Why?"

"Because I didn't keep my word to you," he snarled. "I told you I would stay in control and I...lost it."

"Orson, what are you saying? I was...well, I was enjoying what was happening."

He shook his head. "You don't have to lie. I promise I'll leave you alone."

"For fuck's sake, I'm not lying!" All the hurt and frustration was boiling over, dialed up because none of it made any fucking sense. "I *did* enjoy it. Shit, I would've asked you to stay if you hadn't ran out so fast. If I was lying, I would've made every excuse to get you out the first time you made me..."

Orson's puzzled expression made me trail off, his head cocking to the side. "But I went farther than just using my hands like you said. I...hurt you."

I stared at him, bewildered that we had such opposing perspectives on something we'd both done. "You didn't hurt me. And I didn't mind that you, ah, did more than we discussed. I enjoyed it. A lot."

A frustrated huff left his mouth. "You were pushing me away and telling me to stop."

"Just right in that moment, not for good!" I exclaimed. "I was overly sensitive from coming twice within five minutes!"

The kitchen doors swung open before I'd finished speaking. Sawyer stopped dead in his tracks, then was forced to lean and sway to prevent stacks of cups and saucers from crashing to the floor. Animal reflexes must have kicked in because nothing fell, and he made it to a counter where he swiftly unloaded his burden.

"I heard absolutely nothing," he said, heading straight for the doors again. "And I won't be dropping off more dishes until, oh," he looked at his left wrist, which didn't have a watch, "at least ten minutes. And just to be safe, I won't let anyone else come in either. Great, I'm glad you guys agree. Bye!"

Sawyer disappeared through the doors, leaving Orson and I alone again.

We stared at each other for a few silent moments. I was trying to gauge his reaction while keeping myself together. He ended up cracking first.

Orson's head fell back and he let out a beautiful throaty laugh. His smile was the widest I'd ever seen, and it transformed his face. Sure, he'd had that scowling, moody thing all the time, which was hot in its own way. But seeing his face lit up with joy was breathtaking.

The laughter bubbled out of me in a girlish giggle, and Orson looked even more delighted at the sound.

"I like your laugh," he said.

"Really?" I'd always hated it. I sounded like a toddler when I laughed.

He nodded. "Almost as much as I like the sound of you yelling at me."

I brought a hand to my chest with a mock gasp. "Orson of Howling Death, did you just make a joke?"

"My first attempt. Told you I'm a slow learner."

"Well, it's not the worst joke I've ever heard."

His expression slowly hardened again, and I already missed his smile. "I'm sorry for misunderstanding things that night. I thought you wanted me to stop *everything* and just, you know, leave."

We could always give it another try, was what I wanted to say. Instead I nodded and, desperately needing something to do with my hands, I settled for plucking chamomile flowers one by one from the stash of herbs I'd grabbed.

"It's okay," I said. "I feel like I understand where you're coming from a bit better now."

He didn't crack another smile. If anything, he looked even more tense. "I'm sorry about before too. When I just showed up to install cameras without talking to you first. And how I acted when you spoke to me then. You were the reasonable one. I was not." His gaze lowered, and I could picture his wolf bowing his head in the same gesture, ears and tail down. "I don't mean to be a difficult person, but that's not an excuse. I'm sorry for being an asshole, Shiloh."

Fuck me, I wanted to hug him so badly. I went to him, my feet moving as if of their own volition. The next thing I knew, that icy stare was incredibly close. It was all I could see, and there was warmth there that I hadn't noticed before.

"I forgive you, Orson." My gaze lowered and, damn, his lips were pretty close too. "And I don't think you're difficult or an asshole. Maybe just a bit misunderstood."

His face raised and lowered in a slight nod. "Socializing as a human just doesn't come naturally to me. But I am trying."

"I know you are." I so badly wanted to touch him, to bring him home. Not just for more mind-bending sex, but to talk, cuddle, and learn to understand each other more. Maybe his wolf would let me rub his belly again.

Relief flooded my system, but so did apprehension. We'd turned a new leaf but were also starting over, in a sense. Despite what we'd already done, it felt like we were re-introducing ourselves. Maybe clearing the air was enough for him and he had no intention of repeating our full moon night. He wasn't exactly jumping my bones. But then again, nor was I jumping his.

Then an idea hit me. If this was a do-over, maybe we could also retry the first day we met.

"So." I placed a hand on my hip. "Would you like to come to Stout & Spirit and install those security cameras for me?"

Orson's eyebrows lifted in surprise, then that slow, wolfish smile returned. "I have the owner's permission now?"

"You do. When can you come out?"

He scratched the short beard covering his cheek. "How about tomorrow night?"

"That works perfectly."

The wolf grinned wider. "It's a date."

CHAPTER 13
ORSON

I checked my face in one of my mirrors and immediately felt foolish for doing so. It didn't matter what I looked like. Just because Shiloh and I had a truce between us now didn't mean she was interested in me. We had cleared up our misunderstanding, and that was it. Now I was here, at Stout & Spirit, to do a job. Nothing else.

No matter how much my wolf insisted she was our mate. Now that all obstacles were cleared, he thought now was a perfect opportunity to get up close and bite Shiloh in a visible spot, ideally the neck, so all would know she was ours.

"Not happening," I said aloud, checking my hair once more—just to make sure I didn't look *that* stupid—before walking up to the front door.

After my three knocks, I heard Shiloh call out, "It's open!"

I let myself into the cozy interior which was empty of people, Shiloh included. She had the back door propped open though, and her head poked out through the jambs.

"Hey! Did you have dinner? I'm making a pizza, you want one?"

"Um." I inhaled deeply, picking up the scent of dough, cheese, tomato sauce, and all kinds of meats. My stomach growled in answer. "Sure, if it's no bother to you."

"Not at all, I ended up with extra dough actually. Come on back and pick your toppings."

I set my backpack down on the bar before heading toward the back. Shiloh stood at her island counter, topping her pizza with various items set out in small containers. A fire flickered in an alcove in the brick wall across from her.

"I didn't know you had a pizza oven," I mused.

"Yeah, I pre-make 'em and do a limited menu some-times. It's tough when we get busy though, but with Riley helping, I might be able to serve them more often." Shiloh nodded at a round, naked disk of pizza dough next to the one she was building. "That one's yours. Put whatever you want on it."

I stared at the thing like it was an alien artifact. "I've never made my own pizza before."

"Well, lucky you, you missed the hard part." A smile pulled at her lips, and I got the sense that she was teasing me.

"What's that?"

"Prepping the dough. Stretching it, spinning it. You can get that lesson another time." She went to a small sink and rinsed off her hands, dried them on her apron, then reached for a ladle inside a tub of tomato sauce. "How saucy do you like it?"

"I like a good amount."

"Coming right up."

She ladled a heaping of sauce over the dough, starting

at the center and spiraling outward. There was an artistic flair to how she did it, and I would've been content to watch her all day. After the first ladle emptied though, she held the instrument out to me. "Your turn. Just like how I did."

I took it from her and only noticed then that she still had a thick white bandage around her arm. She'd had it on at the human lodge too, and during the full moon. Come to think of it, the only time I hadn't seen it was my first night here to install the cameras.

"Is that burn healing okay?" I asked, carefully dunking the ladle back in the sauce. "You've been wearing that bandage for a couple weeks, it seems."

Shiloh's mood shifted instantly, going from warm and friendly to tense and closed off. She brought her arm to her chest and looked away from me.

"No, it's not so bad," she said. "I just keep it covered at work so nothing gets into it."

I tried to keep my face neutral, tried to keep fucking calm while I sauced my pizza as the scent of her fear hit me hard. This close to her, she smelled terrified.

Even as she moved away to monitor a cauldron of something simmering on a stove, the potency of that scent made me want to act. To remove all threats to her at any cost. My wolf was furious. Not even pizza could appease him. He wanted blood, and frankly, so did I.

But what could I do if she wouldn't tell me what she was so afraid of?

"Are you sure?" I grabbed a handful of shredded cheese, spreading it over my pizza dough in a spiral pattern like I had with the sauce. "Nobody is...hurting you, or anything?"

Shiloh forced out a laugh, the sound nervous and stilted. "Oh no, nothing like that." She glanced my way while stirring whatever was in her cauldron. "It's sweet of you to ask, though."

Sweet is the last thing I'll be when I find out whoever's got you this scared.

I couldn't force it out of her, though, so I busied myself with pepperoni slices as I thought of a subject change. "Whatcha cooking over there?"

"It's, um, a potion for someone." Shiloh's hand shook ever so slightly as she brought the spoon to her nose for a sniff. "Remember that flower I showed you on the trail? This was what I needed it for."

"I see. What kind of potion is it?"

She gave me a coy smile as she adjusted the heat and returned to stirring. "That's between me and my client, sorry."

"Huh, mysterious." I started adding sliced bell peppers to my pizza. "Is it something Howling Death wouldn't approve of?"

Shiloh didn't answer but frowned as she started intently at the pot, stirring methodically.

"Sorry, guess I still need practice with jokes." Finished with my toppings, I rinsed my hands in the sink.

"No, no, you're fine. It's just..." She rubbed her forehead and sighed. "This recipe is just really tricky to get right, and I'm on a tight deadline for it. I've been making test batches, but that's burning through ingredients really quickly and the client is really demanding..." She gave me a sheepish smile. "It's just been a little stressful."

"Oh, I didn't realize." I dried my hands on a towel. "Can I do anything to help?"

"Actually, um." Shiloh chewed her lip and the sight of it brought forth the memory of kissing her. Like I'd been able to get it out of my head since that night. "I need more silver deadnettle, I'm almost out. Would you mind telling me where you got it?"

"Sure, but it's easier to get it myself," I said. "I can go in the morning."

Shiloh lifted a hand toward me. "No, you don't have to do that. I can go."

"It's a strenuous, multi-day hike for humans. The plant grows way up near the peaks."

Her face fell. "You're serious?"

"Yeah, but don't worry about it. I don't mind getting it for you."

"You're a wolf, not a retriever."

For you, I'll be anything. I swallowed. "It's no problem. And it seems you've got enough on your plate already."

Shiloh looked around the kitchen and scratched her head. "You know what? A multi-day hike might be just what I need to de-stress a little."

My wolf howled and jumped for joy under my skin. "What do you mean?"

"I'll close the bar for a few days. Get out of town to go deep into the woods like the old-school witches did." She smiled. "It'll be nice to get away."

I fought to stifle my protective growl. "Well, you're not going alone."

"My, my. What are we going to do about that? If only there was a big bad wolf to keep me safe *and* knew where to find the plant."

A chuckle rolled out of me, and I rubbed my jaw. "You have a funny way of suggesting I come with you."

She laughed. I desperately wanted more of that sound. "I know it'll be faster and easier if I don't come, but I really want to." She looked exhausted all of a sudden, staring at the cauldron as if it were a ruined pot of soup. "I need to get away from all this."

I didn't exactly know what *all this* entailed, but sparks lit up my chest. My wolf was excited about spending so much uninterrupted time with her. And so was I.

"I'll get some off-road tires put on my bike in the morning," I said. "So we're not on foot the whole time but we can still go at a good pace. I can pick you up here right after."

"That sounds great." Excitement lit up her face, and fuck, she looked gorgeous like that. Even with the shadows of exhaustion under her eyes. My greatest desire was to chase those shadows away for good, if only to see her joy shine through even more.

Some time passed before I realized I was just staring at her. Shiloh turned to her cauldron again and my gaze snapped to my pizza, which was pretty much done.

"Great! I'll, uh, get those cameras up."

"I'll get these in the oven," Shiloh said as I returned to the main serving area. "Help yourself to a beer if you want."

"Thanks. Maybe when I'm done here."

"Pizza and beer go fantastically together." Shiloh grabbed a wooden paddle with a long handle, practically dancing through the kitchen before she stuck the business end under my pie to slide into the fire.

I couldn't stop smiling as I got to work, pulling the camera equipment out of my backpack and setting up on the bar. I couldn't wait for tomorrow. Growing up feral wasn't easy, but there was something comforting about the deep woods. I loved the simplicity of the wilderness. Hunting my own food, letting my animal instincts guide me. It was a part of me I never shared, but I was excited to show it to Shiloh.

What surprised me even more was the fact that I was

enjoying myself now. Right here, with her. I loved the sound of her whistling cheerfully and mumbling some song lyrics as she waltzed around the kitchen. She was cooking food for us while I made the bar safer for her. We were making plans. Hanging out. Doing the most utterly mundane stuff, but I loved it. I was happy here.

Is this what being mated feels like?

Inside my skin, my wolf chased his tail like a total goofball. He was ecstatic to be here too.

I glanced through the open doorway to the kitchen where Shiloh had returned to her cauldron. Her hip cocked out, one hand resting there while she stirred half-heartedly with the other hand. Her smile had disappeared, her eyes growing dull and vacant as she stared at the simmering liquid.

The growl rumbled out of my chest before I could stop it, and I made a throat clearing noise to cover it up. Whatever was scaring her, stressing her out to this degree, I would find out.

And I would chase it across Shyftworld through the forbidden territories of the dragons and the vampires if I had to.

I wouldn't stop until all threats against my mate were eliminated.

CHAPTER 14
SHILOH

I barely slept that night. After Orson installed the cameras, he walked me through downloading an app on my phone to access the live feeds. Then we ate our pizzas, drank beer, and talked well into the night. The hours flew by like no time had passed at all.

It was a lot of small talk, mundane stuff about pizza toppings, technology, and random things from the human world. Conversing with Orson was much easier than I anticipated for someone who wasn't comfortable with socializing. He seemed relaxed and asked plenty of questions about me, my life, and the business. His jokes landed a little awkwardly, but I found it cute and endearing.

By the time he left, my body felt exhausted but my brain would not shut off. I closed up the bar and went to my apartment to the sound of his motorcycle driving away, and immediately began packing clothes and supplies in a weekender bag.

I couldn't stop smiling, even when I realized how ridiculous it was to lay out different outfits to compare. We would be roughing it out in the woods for a few days, it didn't matter if I looked cute or not.

But I did want to look cute. For Orson.

A nervous anticipation filled me just as much excitement. We were about to be alone out in the woods together. For days. What would happen? What did *he* think about all this? He was probably smart enough to pick up that I was bullshitting about the bandage on my arm, but I was grateful that he didn't press it.

All things werewolf-crush aside, a few days out in the woods sounded exactly like what I needed. My home, my bar, everything here reminded me of that dragon shifter. I couldn't relax. I felt like I hadn't even taken a full breath in days. My thoughts were constantly racing about making this potion while keeping my business running with a smile on my face to not arouse suspicion. Not to mention all my social commitments. My volunteering at the equinox feast took up a huge amount of time, and while I usually loved it, this threat hanging over me had sucked all the joy out of celebrating this year.

I was so fucking tired. I needed a vacation.

My Stout & Spirit patrons would just have to find a different watering hole for a few days. They might grumble once they saw the sign on my door, but they would understand. Before I opened the bar, people would drink at their community lodges. If they were feeling fancy, they could head up to one of Helios City's many posh cocktail lounges.

The next morning, I had just locked everything up when Orson's bike came roaring up the road. Sure enough, his steed now sported wide tires with deep treads for off-roading.

"Ready?" Orson put his kickstand down and came over

to help me with my bag. He was wearing dark sunglasses, which was a damn shame. I missed seeing those eyes.

"Let's hit the road!" I pumped a fist in the air, and he laughed while securing my stuff down with bungee cords.

When he resettled in the driver's seat, I didn't hesitate to climb on behind him. He didn't react to my legs pressing on the outside of his, but he startled when my arms came around his waist.

"Sorry!" I jerked my hands back. "Is this okay?"

"Yeah! Yeah, you're totally fine." He put the sunglasses on top of his head, then gave me an adorably shy look over his shoulder. "I guess I've just never had someone on the back of my bike before."

"Well, I'm thrilled to pop your cherry." I gave a couple light pats to his stomach. "I'll be gentle with you."

His laugh was that gorgeous, deep throaty sound. I wanted to press my whole body against his to feel it vibrating through me. But I kept my hold light on his waist as he resumed facing forward.

Orson kicked the bike into motion, and then we were off.

I had only been on a couple rides before with Sawyer and forgotten how much I missed them. This was freeing in a way like nothing else was. How could I be stressed with so much fresh air rushing over my skin? While going so fast with a hot werewolf in front of me?

Before I knew it, my arms had wrapped around Orson's torso as far as they could go and my chin rested on his shoulder. He was relaxed in his seat, taking the turns with ease even as the paved roads turned to dirt and gravel. The gravel gave way to larger stones as we headed deeper into the woods, the path becoming overgrown from lack of maintenance.

Soon, holding tightly onto him became a necessity. All semblance of road or trail disappeared, the off-road tires putting in work as they carried us uphill through wild terrain. Orson maneuvered the bike effortlessly all the way, taking the path of least resistance, which there wasn't much of up here. There was barely any cleared space, but all rocks, shrubs, trees, and debris.

And this was just day one.

Eventually, Orson stopped the bike in a relatively flat area with some large boulders clustered around.

"Might as well stop here for a lunch break." He helped me off the bike first, then swung off himself.

"Sounds good. What are you in the mood for?" I went to my bag and started rifling through it. "Can't really build pizzas out here, but I brought some stuff we can heat over a fire."

I stopped rummaging as a slow smile came to the wolf's face.

"Or I could hunt for us." Orson had left his sunglasses off and his eyes were bright with anticipation. "There's good pheasant out here."

The forest air was cool, but my skin heated at his suggestion. Why was the idea of a man hunting food for us so damn hot? It had been ages since my people had lived in caves, but my inner cavewoman was very much alive and she heartily approved.

"Sure, if it's no trouble," I said. "I haven't had fresh pheasant in years."

"No trouble at all. I'm dying for a good hunt." Orson peeled off his jacket and draped it over the motorcycle. "Be back in under an hour."

He headed off through the brush, and I watched him peel the T-shirt off his body as he walked away. Smooth skin stretched over swaths of muscle. His back stood out amongst all the greenery and rough textures of tree bark and stone. I watched until I couldn't see him anymore, then caught only a flash of silvery-gray fur. A predator in search of prey.

Shifters were so fascinating. Apart *from* the wild in one moment, a part *of* it in the next.

I built a small campfire, then looked around the area for edible plants. I squealed with delight at the discovery of a blackberry bush just a few yards away and gathered as many berries as I could. A few feet away from that, I found a patch of wild arugula and gathered some up to make a salad.

A little cleansing spell was all that was needed to ensure the plants were safe to eat. I spotted Orson's moonlight pelt returning just as I built up the fire to a nice burn and set up a roasting spit over it to cook his hunt.

The silver, icy-eyed wolf came right up to me, laid his kill at my feet, and proudly sat back on his haunches.

"Oh my God, this pheasant is huge!" I inspected the bird, a male in his prime with his signature bold feathers. It looked to be a clean kill too, which I was grateful for. A broken neck with minimal blood. I had no problem butchering animals, but didn't care for carving up already-mangled corpses.

"Good job, Orson! This will last us 'til dinner too."

The wolf whuffed and lifted his head proudly. I reached over to scratch the fur under his jaw and he puffed his chest out farther, lifting his snout all the way to the sky to give a short howl.

I laughed and scratched him more aggressively, coming up to the bases of his ears. "Yes, you are a *very* good boy."

He suddenly lunged forward and licked my nose. The

sudden movement startled me, and I landed on my butt. "Oh, I wasn't expecting that."

I went to scratch him again, but the silver wolf backed away with a soft whimper, head and tail low to the ground. Then he turned, bounding through the brush. I sat there confused, wondering if I had done something wrong. I thought I knew werewolf behavior pretty well from living in their territory all my life, but what did I really know about the human-animal brain?

Orson returned to camp a few minutes later, fully dressed in his jeans and T-shirt while I had gotten started on plucking the bird.

"Everything alright?" I asked as he knelt by the fire.

"Yeah, just." He gave an awkward shrug. "I can't shift with clothes on, you know. Thought I'd spare you from being scarred for life."

I knew that. Again, I knew werewolves pretty damn well for not being one. That wasn't why his wolf had whimpered like he'd been kicked.

I figured it was probably better to let it rest for now, so I returned my attention to pulling feathers. "Thanks again for hunting."

"My pleasure." He nodded at the kill. "Need help with that?"

"I got this. You did the hard work already."

He started to relax then, sitting on a rock and stretching his long, jean-clad legs. "Wasn't *that* hard."

"Oh yeah? Are you humble-bragging?"

"Nah, just bragging."

I laughed, genuinely surprised by his wit. "At least you're honest."

"Usually," he said so low that I almost didn't hear.

I snorted. "Well, that's a loaded answer if I ever heard one."

Orson stared into the fire, his icy gaze a pale backdrop for the flames' reflection. "It's not that I'm *dis*-honest. There are just things about me I'd prefer people to not know."

"Like that you were feral?"

He shook his head and shrugged. "Pretty much everyone knows that. Not much I can do about it."

"Well, I think it's totally fair that you want to keep some things private. Some things are just better kept to yourself, you know?"

He lifted his gaze to stare across the fire at me, mouth pulling into a smirk. "Are you telling me the most popular witch in Vargmore has deep, dark secrets?"

"No." I hoped the simple word came out as casual and not defensive. "But privacy is really important to some people, and I respect that."

"It is." Orson rubbed his arm, going back to looking at the fire. "Sometimes keeping certain knowledge away from people actually protects them. Even if they wouldn't see it that way."

Don't I know it, I thought. It wasn't like I felt the safety of the entire territory rested on my keeping this potion project under wraps or anything.

"Are you secretly mated or something?" I asked on a whim.

Orson sat straight up, his eyes narrowing. "No. Why would you ask me that?"

"Just trying to guess what your big secret is." I gave a small smile. "And to push your buttons just a little."

He relaxed again and let out a huff of breath that sounded very similar to his wolf's. "Are you mated?"

"Me? No, of course not!" Finished with the plucking, I retrieved my knife to make quick work of gutting the bird. "I could never keep a secret like that. The whole territory would be talking about it since I'm so *popular.*"

"Any male would be a fool to keep you a secret anyway," Orson muttered. He was quiet for a while and then said, "So, you and that angel from the bar…"

"Not an item," I said quickly. "He supplies me with beer from his brewery. We have a professional relationship, nothing more."

"He's attracted to you," Orson said, a low growl edging his voice. "I could smell it that night."

"Yeah, you see…" I raked my hand back through my hair. "He'd asked me out earlier that day. I turned him down but said he should hang out while we were open. I guess after a couple drinks, he had enough liquid courage to try again. He was very embarrassed about it and has been nothing but professional since. I trust Kaz, he's not a creep."

"Okay, that's good to hear." Orson stood from his rock and held his hand out to me. "Let's find you a stream to wash up in."

"Wash up? I'm not done yet." I gestured down to the half-cleaned bird.

"Yes, but you've been touching your hair and face while you talk."

I froze, horrified. "Oh my God, are you serious?" As a reflex, I started bringing my hands up to my face before remembering and stopping short.

Orson was trying to hold back a laugh as he gestured at me. "It doesn't look bad, kind of like war paint. But it doesn't seem like your style, so…"

"Shut up." I stood up, holding my bloody, gut-smeared hands away from my body. "Help me find some water."

"You can't smell it?"

"No! I'm not a freaking werewolf!"

He threw his head back and laughed. I joined in, even though I was the butt of the joke.

It was impossible not to. I was having the time of my life with him.

CHAPTER 15

ORSON

After Shiloh's warpaint incident, we cooked the pheasant and ate with a salad she'd gathered and prepared. All the while, we talked and teased each other. Her smiles and laughter were like rewards that I'd gotten greedy for. I wanted them again and again.

Talking to her was easier than any other person I'd ever met, even my packmates. I thought only the male werewolves I was closest to, had the most in common with, were worth talking to. How wrong I was.

This hilarious, smart, gorgeous witch had my wolf in a locked collar to which only she held the chain. He was annoyed that I hadn't kissed her or made any effort to please her since the full moon. The opportunistic bastard waited until my guard was down before he kissed her himself. Licking her face like a damn puppy.

He had yelped with pain because of how hard I yanked back control. It was well after the full moon, so he couldn't wrestle with me for it now. I shouldn't have let him have so much control to begin with, but Shiloh was scratching us so *good.* My animal would have eaten out of her hand, and I would've been on all fours right next to him.

After lunch, we packed up, smothered the fire, and kept heading up the mountain. By my estimate, we'd hit the first peak tomorrow by about mid-day.

With the way Shiloh had wrapped around me on the back of my bike though, I was tempted to do laps around the mountain and extend this trip by a week, if not more. Anything for more time with my witch, more opportunities to collect my trophies of her laughs and smiles.

The ride got bumpier the higher in elevation we went. No set of wheels had touched this terrain in a long time, if ever. This was pure, uncharted wilderness. The air also got colder, thinner. I felt Shiloh's strained breaths in my ear, felt the shivering in her fingers, and my protective instincts roared out to keep her safe from the elements.

"Put your hands under my jacket," I yelled over the engine. "It'll keep you warmer."

The weight of her hands lifted away, and I almost jumped out of my seat when icy fingers brushed over my ribs.

She had gone under my jacket *and* shirt.

"Sorry!" Shiloh yelled. "But we'll both end up warmer this way."

Sweet moon, she had absolutely no reason to be sorry. I'd been craving her touch for so long, I would take anything I got, icicle fingers or not.

Shiloh's torso pressed flush to my back, the side of her face to my shoulder, and her legs cradling mine. She was still shivering, and I brought one of my hands to hers on my stomach.

"We're coming to a good stopping point soon. Then we can warm up properly."

She lifted her head and I heard the smile in her voice as she spoke in my ear. "Sounds like you're insinuating something."

I stole a quick, confused glance over my shoulder. "What? Building a fire?"

Her forehead dropped to the back of my neck, and fuck me, I liked that contact too. "Nevermind, it's nothing."

At dusk, we reached our stopping point, which wasn't so much a cave as it was a sizable indent in the side of a ridge. In any case, it would protect us from the elements to some degree.

I got off the bike, leaving it turned on, and told Shiloh to stay on it as I removed my jacket for her to wear.

"Scoot up to my seat, it'll warm you." I secured the jacket around her shoulders. "Just sit tight while I get a fire ready."

Shiloh scoffed and put her arms through the holes of my jacket as she slid down from the bike. She kept eye contact with me the whole time, lifting her chin the moment her shoes hit the ground. "I'm not that fragile, Orson. And I don't 'sit tight' while others do the work."

She walked off and all I could do was stare.

Did the pretty witch listen to me? No.

Did she turn me the hell on? Absolutely yes.

"By all means, go ahead and build the fire," she said.

"What are you doing?" I asked. She appeared to be searching for something on the ground, carefully turning over stones and nudging fallen branches with her feet.

"I'm going to cast a barrier ward. It'll protect us from any predators and keep the heat from the fire within the barrier."

"Sounds good." I continued watching her, fascinated as she bent down to examine objects from the forest floor.

"But there are no predators. The feral packs won't bother us."

"You're sure they're the ones at the top of the food chain out here?" Shiloh picked up a rock and branch. "No bears? Or bear shifters?"

"If wolves shared this territory with bears, we'd be well and truly fucked." I turned off the bike and started on the fire building.

"You think so?" Shiloh smirked at me as she placed her rock and stick facing south in a seemingly very intentional arrangement. "You couldn't take on a bear shifter?"

"My kind is already fifty percent bigger than standard gray wolves," I said. "Assuming the same logic would go for bear shifters, can you imagine a ten-foot tall grizzly? That might even be underestimating, an alpha male would be at least twelve feet tall."

"You're right," Shiloh chuckled as she arranged more sticks and rocks. "That would be terrifying."

"The wolf packs would be wiped out in a season. Or domesticated, who knows?"

"Your bear overlords will turn you into chihuahuas!" she cackled.

"Now that's just disgraceful," I bit out, which made her laugh even harder. And I soaked up every decibel of that beautiful sound. "Will you tell me how your barrier ward works?" I asked when her laughter faded.

She looked up at me, surprised. "You really want to know?"

I shrugged. "I've always been curious about magic."

"Well, it's similar to how our border territories work," she explained. "We can go in and out of the barrier with no issue, you'll just feel a sensation when it makes contact with your body."

"What do the sticks and rocks do?"

"Those are anchor points in the four cardinal directions —north, south, east, and west. Now, where the magic comes in." She went to the bike and pulled a small cork-capped glass bottle from her bag. "It's a little bit of concentration, moonlight, and asking the earth's magnetic field politely."

Shiloh went to each of the anchor points, whispered some kind of chant, and sprinkled some of the powdery contents of the bottle over the selected sticks and rocks. Once done, she capped the bottle and grinned at me. "Go ahead. Step out of the border by crossing the line between any two anchor points."

I went for a little walk and sure enough, I felt something tangible on my skin as I stepped out of the barrier. It was little more than the soft pressure of a breeze, just enough to be noticeable. Just to see if it would make Shiloh laugh, I hopped in and out of the barrier a few times.

Not only did she laugh, she came over and tugged lightly at my wrist. "Get back here, you goof."

"It's warmer inside here already," I remarked. I had noticed a chill after taking off my jacket, even though shifters naturally ran warm and the cold didn't bother me much. Now, I was comfortable in just my T-shirt despite standing a good ten feet away from the fire.

"I'm just fascinated by this." I stuck only my hand outside the barrier this time, feeling like I was reaching into a freezer. "You're quite the crafty witch."

"Nah." Shiloh went to unpack more things from the bike. "I'm pretty standard issue actually. A child witch can make simple barriers. It's one of the first things they're taught."

"I see." I went to help her unpack, laying out our leftover pheasant next to the fire while I set up the roasting spit to reheat them. "So you're used to having magic-wielders around? No freshly-immigrated humans in your family?"

"No," Shiloh sighed. "My family were among the first witches in Vargmore. I didn't even know there were people who couldn't shift or use magic until I went to school with human children."

"The moon magic is powerful in you then."

"You would think." She sounded a bit sad. "Moon magic is all about cycles. Ebbs and flows, waxings and wanings. A lot of it is deeply tied to fertility. Both in the growth and abundance of the land, and also," she spread her hands, "in terms of people and animals. Reproducing, you know."

"Okay." I got the sense she was trying to explain something to me, and I made sure to listen.

"I come from a long, powerful line, yes. But my mother was...well, cursed is probably the best term for it."

"Cursed?"

Shiloh nodded, keeping her eyes away from mind as she set up for dinner. "During the werewolf conflict with the vampires, my mother was found to be helping dragon shifters escape to the human world."

"That *would* cause an uproar these days," I admitted. "But I'm sure she had her reasons. Were the wolves and dragons even enemies back then?"

"It was right after the dragons made their support of the vampires clear. So yes, it was an act of betrayal to be helping them instead of the werewolves. So her moon magic was stripped from her in what I'm told is a very painful ordeal. Drink?"

She held out a flask to me, which I accepted, and she continued her story.

"Without moon magic, my mother found it very diffi-cult to get pregnant. But surprise!" Shiloh lifted her arms in mock celebration. "She had me, her miracle baby. But her lack of moon magic also made her more susceptible to infection, and she passed away weeks after I was born. So, long story short, the whole witch community raised me."

"Damn." I took a fast sip of the liquor in her flask, rye whiskey by the taste of it, and handed it back to her. "Sorry about your mother."

Shiloh shrugged as she accepted the flask. "Thanks, although I never knew her enough to mourn, you know? While I'm grateful for the ones that did raise me, they all made it very well-known how much they despised my mother. How she came from such a great, powerful line and threw it all away. And that created a different kind of barrier, you know?" She upturned the flask and took a long swig. "I was so scared as a kid that I would be punished for what my mom did. Even as an adult, I sometimes wonder if people think I'm gonna betray the territory." Her bandaged hand shook as she took another drink. "I guess that's why I've tried so hard to be involved in the community. Running the bar, helping with the human festivals and other events. It's like I'm trying to atone for my mother's sins."

"You don't need to atone for anything," I said. "Everyone here loves you. And they know that you love Vargmore."

"Everyone, huh?" She cocked her head and gave me a smile that left me thoroughly tongue-tied. "What about your family?"

"I don't have many alive," I admitted, accepting the flask from her again. "The few that are, aren't worth talking about. A bunch of scumbags."

"Really?" Shiloh's brow furrowed. "You mean the feral wolves?"

"They're not my family. Like you, they're the community who raised me. Well…" I paused with the flask on the way to my lips, wondering about how much I should tell her. "I have a half-sister who's still feral. She's more civilized than most of them actually, and I worry about her sometimes."

"An outcast among outcasts, huh?"

"Yes. She and I kind of bonded over that. I also worry about her being able to survive out in the wild."

"Because of how harsh the wilderness is?"

"That, along with the fact that she can't shift."

Shiloh's eyebrows went up into her hairline. "Can't shift? So she's human?"

"She looks it, but no, there's a wolf in there. She just can't draw it out for some reason. What worries me is that she can't defend herself. She's vulnerable, even a liability out here, to be honest." I took a swing of the flask. "I tried to get her to come with me when Tryn brought me into Howling Death, but she refused."

"Would you want to pay her a visit while we're out here?"

"Probably shouldn't. Ferals don't like talking to civilians much."

"That's understandable. It's too bad though, if she's the only family you got."

"The only one that matters, anyhow." I returned the flask to her. "You hungry?"

"Starving," she groaned, running a hand across her belly.

"Let's eat then."

We ate our leftover pheasant while talking over less serious topics.

When Shiloh started yawning and her eyelids got droopy, I stood up and looked around for some privacy.

"I'll be in my wolf form during the night," I told Shiloh. "Just as a precaution. He'll awaken easily if something sneaks up on us."

"Works for me." The pretty witch was half-asleep already, rolling out her sleeping bag and shaking out her blanket.

I fed another couple of logs to the fire before heading off for some privacy to shift. When I returned, Shiloh was already reclined and bundled up, the firelight dancing over her relaxed features. She was facing the fire, so I padded around to guard her back, facing the barrier she'd made.

I plopped down and rested my chin on my paws, turning my nose toward her hair to pick up some of that orange-cinnamon scent. Just as I started to drift off, Shiloh rolled over, her hand outstretched and sinking into the fur at my shoulder.

"Goodnight, Orson," she whispered.

CHAPTER 16
SHILOH

I woke up hugging a space heater. Or at least, that was what it felt like. The bank of warmth against my torso and cheek kept me in a lulled, drowsy state I didn't want to emerge from. My eyes hadn't opened yet, and I was *so* comfortable.

It wasn't until my palm slid to a more comfortable position on this space heater that I realized it felt like skin. A warm body.

I snatched my hand away like it had been on a burning stove and my eyes popped open. Oh sweet moon, I'd hoped I was wrong, but no. A very human, very naked Orson lay on his side, still asleep. And I was pressed up against his back, spooning him under the blanket.

"Fuck." Now wide awake, I scooted away from him as discreetly as I could, but the moment my body was no longer in contact with his, the werewolf began to stir.

Orson rolled to his back and rubbed his face with a groan. Then he pulled his hands away and stared at fingers, blinking rapidly.

"Good morning," I said awkwardly.

He sat up abruptly, taking care to stay covered from the waist down. "Why am I human?"

"You must have shifted back in your sleep," I said. "I woke up and covered you with a blanket so you'd stay warm." *And then I spooned you at some point while I was sleeping.* Probably best to keep that to myself.

Orson groaned again and returned to rubbing sleep out of his eyes. "Sorry about that. I'm not usually a sleep-shifter."

"Nothing to be sorry for." I slid out from under the blanket we'd ended up sharing, hating the loss of warmth from our combined body heat. "I'll get some coffee started."

It was an excuse to get my head on straight and also to give him some privacy to get dressed. *Don't turn around,* I thought as I heard the rustling of clothes behind me. *Don't be a perv.*

"We should reach the summit of the first peak today." Orson's voice floated from behind me before he entered my field of vision, wearing his white T-shirt and faded jeans as he sat in front of the fire. "Should only take a couple hours," he added, rubbing his palms together before holding them out toward the fire.

"How much of the plant was left?" I walked around the fire with two mugs of coffee and handed one to him. "When you left last time."

"There were maybe a dozen shrubs I saw spread out over the spot I was in. I just dug up one so I could carry it back down in my jaws."

I tried to do some quick math in my head. Would a dozen shrubs of deadnettle even be enough for the amount the dragon wanted? I needed the leaves and flowers of the plant. Even if I perfected the recipe with the next test batch, which was doubtful, I had used that entire first shrub already. Could I scale up the recipe and still have the right amount?

A potion as volatile as this one needed to be exact in every way. It wasn't some everyday concoction that I could use substitutions for.

"Shiloh?" Orson cocked his head at me. "You okay?"

"Yeah," I said with false cheer. "Yeah, great." My coffee was still at a scalding temperature but I forced a mouthful down. "Just antsy to get going, that's all."

)))))) ((((((

THE MOUNTAIN'S summit was bright and sunny, though still bitterly cold. Patches of snow remained stubbornly at the base of trees and on the shadowy sides of boulders. In the distance, more snow covered the higher peaks of the mountain range. This peak was the smallest, but it was still the highest elevation I'd ever been in the territory.

All the untouched wilderness was absolutely breathtaking. As Orson drove us, I wished I could be here just to enjoy it. I wished our time together in this place of pure, wild magic wasn't tainted by the looming presence of the dragon shifter at my back.

"Not much farther," Orson yelled at me over the grinding, high gears of his engine. "There's a meadow up ahead with your plants bordering it."

I nodded, placing my cheek on the back of his shoulder. He clasped one of his hands over mine, lacing our fingers. I returned the squeeze, allowing the smile on my lips and the fluttering sensation in my chest. This werewolf just seemed to know that I needed some comfort, some reassurance that everything would be okay. I appreciated the affection from him, especially as someone who claimed to be so socially unaware. Somehow, he knew what I needed without words.

"It's crazy to me that the deadnettle is up this high," I said when we reached a patch of flatter terrain and his bike quieted down. "How did the early witches find it? I doubt many of them trekked this far up the mountain."

"The feral packs tell stories of an ice age roughly a thousand years ago," Orson answered. "They said nearly all of Vargmore was covered in snow, and Shadowburn Cliffs was once a rainforest."

"What? I can't even imagine that." Shadowburn Cliffs, the dragon territory, had always been a scorching desert as far as I knew.

"If there's any truth to it, your plant probably grew at lower elevations back when the recipe was developed. So it would have been more accessible back then."

It was a good theory, and it likely explained why silver deadnettle was believed to have gone extinct in the last few decades. Weather systems had probably shifted dramatically in the last thousand years. The Vargmore witch community kept meticulous historical records, but I never thought much about cracking open those ancient tomes until now. Recent history was everyone's main concern these days—the formation of the four territories and the conflicts and alliances that created those borders.

"There's the meadow." Orson unlinked our fingers to point, and I missed the connection. But then he grabbed my hand again, and the fluttering in my chest returned.

We drove around the edge of the meadow, and I recognized the general shape of the shrubs bordering that side. But something wasn't right.

When Orson stopped the bike, I didn't wait for him before hopping off. I went right up the nearest plant and felt dread pooling in my stomach as I examined the branches.

"There's no flowers," I said in a stunned whisper. "Where are the flowers? Did they fall off?"

I dropped to my haunches and ran a hand over the ground at the plant's base. All the leaf litter matched the nearby trees and grass growing, but not the shrub.

"Where are the flowers?" Panic entered my voice as I re-examined the naked, woody shrub. "They didn't fall, where are they?"

Orson came up next to me and pinched one of the branches before he leaned down to smell it. "Looks like they've been eaten. Probably by the elk or mountain goats that live up here."

"No, no, no. I *need* the flowers. There won't be enough." I went to each plant, examining it one by one. A few still had most of their flowers intact, but it would be nowhere near enough. Some of them had new buds forming, but that wouldn't help either. I needed to harvest it at the full-grown, mature stage.

"Fuck, what am I gonna do? It's not enough."

"Will a new set of flowers grow back?" Bless Orson for trying to be helpful.

I shook my head. "No, not likely. The grimoire said they flower once a season. This is it for them."

This was the worst possible scenario. Even if I figured out the right proportions to the recipe immediately upon returning home and made a full batch, it needed a week to cure. That would put me right at my end-of-the-month deadline with the dragon shifter.

There was no way I'd meet the deadline now. I was well and truly fucked.

And so was the entire territory.

"Is there anywhere else?" I asked Orson. "Anywhere else on the mountain where these grow?"

"I'm not sure, but we can look." Not that I could focus on his face much, but he was looking at me strangely. "It's going to be okay, Shiloh."

"No." I shook my head, my vision blurring with tears of my failure, tears for all of the people who wouldn't be saved. "It's not. It's not okay, it was never okay. I couldn't do it, I couldn't..."

My panicked muttering was smothered by the lapel of a leather jacket. I was pressed against a warm, hard wall that smelled wonderful. A heavy weight rested on the back of my head while another ran up and down my back.

"Tell me what's going on, Shiloh," Orson growled in my ear. "Tell me who's got you so scared."

"I can't—I mean...it's no one." My face pressed into the center of Orson's chest, his heartbeat an insistent pounding against my cheek.

"Little witch, your scent is all fear." Orson's hand on the back of my head curled into a fist, trapping some of my hair in his grip. "Let me help you. Let me protect you."

"You can't," I whimpered into his shirt. "There's nothing you can do."

The growl rattling out of his chest was one of frustration. "Shiloh, don't write me off before you give me a chance."

The weight of that sentence felt heavy, like it carried more than one meaning. I lifted my head to meet his eyes, my exhausted, broken-down soul daring to hope. To find another soul just like it, to not only share this burden with but to shelter with me from the fallout that would surely come.

"What do you mean by that, Orson?" I asked in a whisper.

His fist released my hair, the hand opening to cup my neck and run his thumb along my cheekbone. I leaned into the weight of his hand, the support of it so tender and badly needed that I wanted to cry again.

"You don't have to fight all your battles alone." His forehead brushed mine and warm air from his mouth teased my lips. "My teeth and claws are yours, Shiloh. Whoever is scaring you, hurting you, let me be your weapon to annihilate them."

The strength of my voice was gone, a weak whisper as I said, "I can't—"

"Please." Orson cupped my face with both hands now, his thumbs brushing the edges of my lips. "My wolf will never so much as break a hair on your head, but he wants blood, Shiloh. He's howling at me right now to protect you. And I'm in full agreement with him. We are bound to you, my sweet witch."

Somehow, despite my heart pounding like a drum and my body taking on a floating sensation at his words, I found my voice.

"I can't let you get hurt."

"They've already hurt you," Orson growled. He dropped one hand to my bandaged forearm. "That's what this is, isn't it? I could smell your fear every time I asked you about it."

"Orson, please," I whimpered. "I don't want you to get caught in the crossfire."

"Too bad. I'll walk through dragonfire to make sure you're safe."

I shook my head and a sob wracked through me, the mental image of that last statement too much to bear.

Orson stiffened. "Is that who it is, a dragon shifter? Are they forcing you to make this potion?"

I could only cry harder in response, the emotional toll of everything releasing like a broken dam. I hated that I wasn't strong enough to hold it all in, to keep Orson from being involved.

"Shiloh." Both of his strong arms went around me, pressing me flush to his chest. "We have to tell Derric."

"No!" I lifted my head. Any other time, I never would have let him see my puffy, red crying face, but this was too important. "He'll burn the entire territory if anyone finds out. It's bad enough that you know, but Howling Death cannot retaliate. People will die."

"Dragons can't be allowed to just waltz into our territory and make threats," Orson snarled back. "They can't force people to make potions for...what, exactly? What does the potion do, Shiloh?"

I returned my forehead to his chest, shaking my head back and forth. I wished I could rewind time, go back to yesterday or even the day before. Pizza, beer, and flirting in my empty bar, when Orson was none the wiser and this secret was my burden alone to bear. Back then, I at least wholeheartedly believed I was keeping Vargmore safe.

Now, I couldn't help but think I'd doomed my home and all the people in it.

"Shiloh, please." Orson ran his hands up and down in broad sweeps over my back. "Talk to me. Don't shut me out. Don't deal with this alone."

He placed a kiss on the top of my head and pulled me in tighter, which dragged another ugly sob out of my throat. I was so damn tired of dealing with this all on my own, but the risk was not worth it. These new sides of him that I was just discovering—the sweetness and vulnerability, his dorky but adorable sense of humor, none of this would last if that dragon came through on his threats.

"You know why that dragon came to you?" Orson's chest vibrated against my forehead. "Because he was too chickenshit to confront Howling Death directly. He targeted a lone witch because being underhanded and sneaky gave him an advantage. Against a whole pack, he'd have no chance. He's a coward, Shiloh. So let me and my pack chase that overgrown lizard away for good."

Orson brought his head down, nuzzling his cheek against my temple. "Let me prove myself as a worthy protector for my mate."

My head jerked up and I backed away as if he'd shoved me, a sudden jolt of energy making me stumble. "What... did you say?"

CHAPTER 17

SHILOH

Orson's expression was raw, open, and hiding nothing at all. He believed what he'd said wholeheartedly and was laying it all out on the line.

"My mate," he repeated softly. "My wolf has known since the beginning. It's just...taken the human side of me this long to come around, I guess."

I opened my mouth to deny it but found myself physically incapable of saying the words. I wasn't of his kind, but werewolf and witch pairings weren't *that* unusual. Moon magic was said to have been guided by fate, and right now? I couldn't help but feel like fate had sent me someone when I needed them most.

Not *just* someone but this werewolf in particular. A wolf I thought I hated but could never stop thinking about.

"The night of the full moon," I whispered. "It was you that I needed. Not just any person, but you specifically."

Orson nodded tentatively, his throat bobbing with a swallow. "I followed your scent after my run with the pack.

No one else could smell it as strongly. It was like you were calling to me."

A moan left my mouth as my skin heated, my core hollowing out as if on command. Orson's nostrils flared, his lips curling in a possessive growl. "Are you doing that on purpose?"

"Doing what?"

"Your scent is...blooming. Fuck, I'm sorry. It's making me..."

He turned to adjust himself, but I grabbed his forearm. "Orson."

"Shiloh?" The way he said my name, on a tight breath like he was already inside me, sent the pulse between my legs pounding. He waited, frozen, like what I was about to say might shatter him.

"I don't want to be alone," I whispered. "But if anything happened to you, I—"

"Sweet witch, don't worry about me." His hand returned to my face, a warm, rough palm against my cold cheek. "I am never just one wolf. My pack will answer your call for help." Another low, rumbling growl left his throat. "But I will be the one to tear this dragon's throat out. I promise you that."

"Because I'm your...mate?" The word sent a gentle tingle through me, speeding up my heart and lighting up the nerves under my skin.

"Because you deserve nothing less."

I didn't know who kissed who first. Our mouths locked together in the middle, in perfect sync. The aching need that had been reduced to low-burning embers since the full moon now roared to life in an inferno. Orson grabbed me around the waist, anchoring my hips to his as he plundered my mouth. I felt the erection he'd been trying to hide a moment ago against my lower belly, and my hips rolled instinctively against him.

"Mm, Shiloh," he groaned against my mouth before catching my lips in another kiss. "What do you want me to—"

"Everything," I panted. "Don't ever stop, I want it all. No boundaries. I want all of you."

"Even a bite?" He dragged a kiss along my jaw, nipping his way to my earlobe. "My wolf wants to mark you as ours. But I can wait, if you want me to."

That thought was sobering. A bite sealed the mating bond forever. I knew I wanted right now. I wanted his help, his pack, and hell yes I wanted him inside me. But a mating bite?

"Yes, let's wait on that," I agreed. "But I want everything else."

"My 'everything else' is yours." Orson smirked as he dropped low, wrapped his arms around my thighs, and lifted me up.

With a laugh, I grabbed his shoulders for support. "Where are you taking me?"

"My bike."

I landed gently on a cushioned seat a few seconds later, and Orson wasted no time drawing my legs apart so he could step between them and kiss me again. "Figured you'd be more comfortable here," he murmured, running his hands up my thighs.

"I don't want to be comfortable."

He frowned. "No?"

"I want to be impaled on your cock and screaming until I don't have a voice anymore."

His chuckle was low and pleased. "Leave it to fate to bring a wild witch and a feral wolf together like this."

"Stop talking and start fucking me." Yes, maybe I was dying for a distraction and some stress relief from my shitty situation. But I also just urgently needed him. This felt just like the full moon, except my head was much clearer. All my desire and frustrating attraction to Orson suddenly made sense. *We* made sense.

He smothered my mouth in another deep kiss, his chuckle turning into a moan as I rubbed the length of him through his jeans. Warm, rough hands slid under my jacket and then layers of shirts until he reached my bare skin. His touch was like a brand, searing himself into me everywhere he passed over.

"Cold?" he asked between kisses.

Our breaths formed clouds when we exhaled, so it must have been cold out here in the woods, but I felt none of it.

"No, please don't stop."

"Not on your life, sweet witch."

He removed his hands from me only to peel away his own layers of jacket and T-shirt. Then he returned to me, baring my skin to the cold, wild air and his hands, his skin. Even as a semi-feral werewolf about to get some action, he was considerate enough to keep my clothes draped over the handlebars of his bike instead of discarding them on the ground.

Orson wrapped me in a hug, strong forearms braced against my back, his chest and abs a firm, hot wall against my breasts and stomach. He gave a small tug on my hair to tilt my face up to his for a kiss. "Good?" he asked.

"Fucking moon, you really are a space heater." I slid my hands around to his back, which was just as warm as his front. There was practically steam rising off his skin.

Orson laughed and kissed the bridge of my nose. "Shifters run hot. But you..." He leaned back and gave me a long appreciative look. "I have no words. You're the most stunning creature I've ever set eyes on."

It was impossible not to melt under the compliment, especially with the unguarded sincerity in his face.

"So are you." I drank him in, the wide shoulders, the thick arms and clearly defined muscle covering every square inch of him. The lips that were built for kissing mine, and of course, those eyes. "Where did your eyes come from?" I blurted out. "I mean, did you get them from your mom or dad's side?"

"Father," he said before kissing me again. "But he's a piece of shit I'd rather not talk about right now."

"Fair enough." I closed my eyes to savor the taste of his mouth, the pressure of his tongue and light nips of his teeth. Meanwhile, I used my sense of touch to get him out of his jeans, finding that hard bulge with my fingers and pulling apart the zipper and button in my way. His reaction when I finally dipped into his boxers and palmed him was glorious.

"Oh fucking *moon...*" Orson's head tilted back like he was going to start howling right then and there. But he righted himself, bringing his forehead to mine as he rolled his hips, thrusting through my grip. "You feel so good, Shiloh."

"Easy, wolfman," I laughed. "I've barely gotten started with you."

"You're already the end of me." His hands went to my waistband and with little effort, he shimmied my pants over my hips and peeled them down my legs. I kicked off my shoes so he could finish the job, then I was completely bare before him.

Orson resumed his spot standing between my legs, even lifting my thighs so I could wrap them around his waist.

"Tell me if you get cold." His mouth ran down the side of my neck, steady hands holding me in place on the seat of his motorcycle.

"I'm fine. Just don't go anywhere." My hands went to his shoulders for balance. He was so strong, solid like the ground supporting us.

"Never." He growled it on a promise while one hand caressed over my hip and ventured down between my legs.

Orson found my clit with no direction, his thumb stroking over the aching bud in a rhythm that left me gasping and squirming. I squeezed around his shaft in return, stroking up the rigid column as I imagined him pressing inside me.

"Orson, please," I whimpered, bucking against his hand. "I need you."

"You're going to come for me first, little witch," he purred.

You'd think he'd be eager to get inside me just as much, but the werewolf took his sweet time playing with me. Orson dipped two fingers into me and stroked just enough to get me going, then he pulled them out to rub my wetness over my clit, making his touch even more slippery. My breath came in rough pants, the tension building up to a single point...and he pulled away to thrust his fingers inside me again.

"Fucking moon, you're killing me," I whined.

"I've barely gotten started with you." He threw my own words back at me with a wolfish grin, which grew wider as I moaned and shook. He was fingering me in *just* the perfect spot, the rough pads of his fingertips curled up and hitting me there again and again...

When he withdrew his hand, I wanted to scream in frustration, not ecstasy. "I can't come if you keep stopping!"

This time, he painted my nipples, making them glossy in the wetness from my pussy before leaning down to suck the tips into his mouth. Orson caressed down my belly to strum my clit again, and I couldn't find it in me to complain. Not with him working so hard with his hand *and* mouth.

He was still hard in my fist, and when he started leaking precum, I followed his lead, spreading the wetness over the most sensitive, male part of him. Orson moaned with his mouth still around my nipple, and I yelped when his teeth grazed the sensitive tip.

When he released me with a pop of his mouth, he straightened to full height, his gaze smoldering like a blue flame. "I just can't get enough of your taste," he groaned, plunging his fingers inside me again. "It drives me just as wild now as it did that night."

"I wanted to touch you here that night." I squeezed his blunt head on an upward stroke. "I would've fucked you back then too."

"I wanted to feel you come on my tongue until my jaw went numb." His fingers found that spot inside me once again, and this time, his thumb went to work on my slickened clit, all digits working in tandem toward a single goal. He didn't pull back this time, didn't tease. Orson drove me headfirst toward the peak like a motorcycle on rocket fuel. With no brakes.

All of the edging he'd done to me earlier culminated into an explosive release, locking up all my muscles as the energy was wrung out of me. Magic even sparked at my fingertips. My consciousness seemed to leave my body and enter a new plane of existence. In my darkened vision, I even thought I saw a city in the distance. Maybe I had just gotten my first peek at the human world.

I blinked and found myself back in my body, staring into a pair of arctic blue eyes with the pupils blown wide. Orson stared wondrously at me, like he was both in awe and immensely pleased.

"You are nothing short of incredible." At least, that was what I thought he said. My pulse was pounding so hard in my ears, my brain still fuzzy as I came down from the most intense orgasm of my life.

Orson withdrew his fingers, leaving me empty as he dragged the hot tips up my body. He reached the hollow of my throat before bringing them to his mouth once again.

"You like my taste that much?" I panted.

"I do." He leaned in, lips glossy from my juices. "You taste like you were made for me."

"That's sweet, but," I grabbed the edges of his pants, hanging low on his thighs, "I need to find out if you fit inside me like you were made for me."

"So do I," he groaned, giving in to my pulls until my thighs were snug around his trim waist and his cock rested on my lower belly. Even against my orgasm-heated skin, he was hot and pulsing. "Take me," Orson said. "Put me where you want me."

He didn't have to ask me twice. I tilted my hips, angled him toward my entrance, and let him slide in.

"Fuck," Orson cursed. He'd started slow but quickly pressed all the way in, filling me to the brim with a gasp.

"Mm, perfect fit." I ran my nails over his ribs, running them down to his perky ass to encourage him to thrust.

"You're perfect." Orson's forehead rested on mine as he started moving in slow but deep rolls of his hips. "Fuck, you're so soft. But you're gripping me like...it's so much better than, I mean, fuck, you just feel so good."

His babbling was adorable, and a laugh rose out of me as I kissed under his jaw.

"What's funny?" he asked.

"Nothing. I'm not laughing at you, you're just so cute."

"Cute, huh?" His hips jacked forward, crashing into me with a hard slap. "Seems I'm not fucking you hard enough."

"You...oh, fuck...you can be both..." The strength he was putting into his thrusts was making it hard to concentrate on anything beside how perfectly he filled me. His increased speed and friction was already building me up to another orgasm.

"I'll be your cute werewolf later," Orson bit out through gritted teeth. "But right now, I'm taking my mate. Giving her the fucking she's been begging me for."

"Yes," I cried out, holding onto his waist, his arms flexed with muscle, the motorcycle, anything I could to hold myself in place as he drove into me again and again.

Orson's hips crashed into my spread-open thighs, his abs flexing hypnotically with every press forward and pull back. Fuck, he was just beautiful to watch, an erotic sight even if I wasn't the one currently being fucked by him. But I was, and that made me the luckiest damn witch in Vargmore.

His rhythm didn't shift in the slightest when his thumb returned to my clit, and I knew it would be game over for me soon. All of my senses were leading me straight toward another orgasm. The touch of him stroking inside me and rubbing my pleasure center on the outside. The sight of him, muscles hard and defined as he thrust into me fluidly. And fucking moon, the sounds he made. Just his ragged breaths, moans, and muttered curses alone added a whole new level of eroticism to it all. I never imagined men making noise would be a thing for me but with Orson, it absolutely was.

He knew I was on the edge the moment it happened. I was trembling with the onset of release, my breath tight in my chest. Orson gave me a tender kiss while he continued to work me with his cock and his fingers.

"Be a good girl and come for me, Shiloh."

Fuck me, that did it.

I never thought I'd be one to come on command, but being with your fated mate hits different. Being with Orson was different.

My body locked up again, and this time, I didn't know if I took another little peek into the human world because my eyes were squeezed shut from the intensity. I couldn't tell up from down, so I clung to my strong, incredible mate as my orgasm squeezed around his thick cock in pulsing waves.

Just when I started to come down, Orson's body tensed on a strangled gasp, and he pressed into me as far as he could go. I felt the swelling and spilling heat of his own release, which only seemed to drag my pleasure out longer.

We stayed connected, leaning on each other with our flagging strength. My head came to his shoulder, and he rested his chin on top of my head.

"Come back to the lodge with me," he said softly after a few moments of quiet. "Stay with me until we know you're safe."

I nodded against his shoulder. "Until everyone is safe."

CHAPTER 18
ORSON

Shiloh and I left the mountain empty-handed. After we got redressed and went for a little walk into the meadow, she took one final look at the plant she'd intended to gather and said, "Fuck the potion."

I couldn't agree more. She still hadn't told me what it would be used for, but I figured we'd get all that information once we sat down with Derric and the rest of Howling Death. While packing up to head back down the mountain, she'd tentatively agreed that we needed to alert the pack.

I hated that this dragon bastard had scared her into not seeking help, made her feel like she had to do this impossible task alone. The sooner that scaly asshole was caught, the better.

The ride back into town was much too short, even if it did take a full day and a half. I loved the feel of Shiloh riding with me, her head on the back of my shoulder, arms holding me for support, fingers idly stroking my chest. I never wanted the ride to end.

As we came up to the Howling Death lodge, I started warming up to the idea of getting off the bike only because

I could soon have Shiloh in my bed. It wasn't even about sex; my instincts were hellbent on providing a safe, comfortable place for my mate. Would my blankets and pillows be soft enough? Next time I washed them, I was going to dump a gallon of fabric softener in there. And then I'd wrap her in them until her scent was permanently embedded in the fibers. I should also double-check the seal on the window to make sure there'd be no cold drafts in the room.

A tall figure was chopping wood in front of the lodge when we pulled up. I scented Derric in the air, and the long hair tied up messily and scarred back confirmed it. Without meaning to, my lip curled up in a snarl. Did he have to be doing that right now? Without a shirt on?

The alpha turned around and gave us a wave, resting the long handle of the axe along the back of his shoulders. "Hey, you two. Have a nice getaway?"

In the old days, it was said that alpha werewolves could have their pick of females in the pack, and it didn't matter if their choices were mated or not. If that were still in practice, Derric would have no protests from whomever he picked. The scars covering him only added to his appeal. They were his trophies, his hard-won reminders of why he led Howling Death. Instead of growing fat on a throne with a crown on his head, Derric kept his position by remaining a well-honed weapon.

His pups, whenever he had them, would be the future leaders of Vargmore, the closest thing werewolves had to royalty. Naturally, females gravitated to him like bees to honey. And right then, I was getting really fucking antsy about him walking closer to my mate.

Looking like a fucking lumberjack, no less. Bastard.

"We did have a nice time." Shiloh tightened her

embrace around me, linking her hands together on my stomach. She sounded tired, and I felt her cheek rub the back of my shoulder. I inhaled discreetly and she did not smell aroused.

Thank the moon.

"Shiloh told me something we need to discuss with the whole pack," I said.

Derric stared at me, his whole body tensing. "Something wrong?"

I placed my hand over Shiloh's. "Yes, a dragon shifter has been threatening her. Threatening the whole territory."

The alpha's lips pulled back, his eyes flashing gold as he growled. "When did this happen?"

"He first came a few weeks ago," Shiloh said in a small voice.

"And you didn't alert us?" Derric demanded.

"She was scared," I growled back. It was a serious risk snapping back at my alpha like that, but for Shiloh, I'd never hesitate. "He threatened to burn the territory if she didn't do what he asked. This isn't her fault, alpha. He cornered her."

Derric backed off, his face relaxing into a controlled mask. "I understand. I'm sorry, Shiloh. Would you be able to tell us everything now?"

I squeezed Shiloh's hand, hoping to give her strength, some encouragement. She squeezed back, her whole body curling around my back like she was seeking out my protection. I'd never felt more proud to be her mate. *Sweet moon, don't let me let her down.*

"Yes," Shiloh answered in a small voice. "I just want him to be stopped."

"Thank you." Derric gave a curt nod at me. "Alert the

whole pack, and tell them it's urgent. We're tackling this right now."

>)>>>》&《《《《(《

TWENTY MINUTES LATER, we were in the great room of the Howling Death lodge, surrounded by the whole pack. Tables and chairs were dragged out from the dining area, since this was more of a pack meeting than someone coming to petition Derric directly.

Shiloh was directed to sit at the center of the biggest table, and I remained glued to her side the whole time. If anyone was surprised that I was acting like a protective mate, none of them said shit. Even Sawyer, who I knew had been close with Shiloh at some point, wisely kept his distance.

Only Tryn came up to me after greeting Shiloh briefly. He clapped me on the shoulder and whispered in my ear, "Mated looks good on you, friend."

I shook my head as he walked away chuckling. Of course he'd know before the mating bites even happened. Shit, he'd probably known for months already. Damn prophetic wolf.

"Thank you all for coming." From the head of the table, Derric's voice projected over the low murmurs and barks of conversation. "There's been a report of a dragon shifter threatening the territory."

Angry growls and howls erupted before he could go on any further. While our kind didn't directly have a history of conflict with dragons, they almost always sided with the vampires, who we did have an ugly, bloody past with.

"Fuck those flying lizards!" someone yelled, earning a chorus of barks and howls in support.

"Shut your muzzles!" yelled Ruse, Derric's VP and second in command. "We have to come up with a plan, mutts!"

When that didn't work, Derric got up from his chair, jumped onto the table, and let out a shrill whistle that hurt everyone's ears. Even Shiloh, who didn't have an ounce of canine in her, winced at the sound.

"The way we all feel about dragons is not news to me," he said. "So save your moaning and *listen* before you jump in with your opinions. No howls, not even a squeak, until Shiloh is done talking." He stepped off the table, landing gracefully on the floor before nodding at her. "The floor is yours whenever you're ready."

"Thank you, Alpha," she said shakily.

I rubbed her back for support, keeping my gaze fixated on her profile. If she gave me a single glance, released a single breath that seemed like she wanted out of here, I'd whisk her away to my room without a second thought.

But my mate was brave. She took a deep breath, then lifted her chin as she began to tell her story.

Right off the bat, I was dying to tear into some scaly dragon's throat. It turned out he first came to her that same night I had been there for the security cameras. Fucking dragon must have watched me, waited for me to leave, and stayed downwind so I wouldn't scent him.

Shiloh unwrapped the bandage around her arm and I wanted to break the table in half over what she revealed. A long black mark, raised up from her skin. She said it burned when the dragon was near, and she believed he used it to track her, keep her on a leash of some sort.

Across the room, no one was looking at Sawyer as he

noticeably paled. The Howling Death enforcer stacked his palms in front of him, hiding his own mark that looked identical to Shiloh's. I glared at him, hoping he could feel my stare. Whatever business he had with dragons, he was certainly in no hurry to talk about it. He'd better hope, for his own sake, that he didn't have anything to do with these threats against my mate.

"Thank you for coming to us with this," Derric said, which was when I realized Shiloh had finished. "I have some follow-up questions, if you don't mind."

"Of course." Shiloh nodded.

"Did this dragon shifter ever tell you his name? Or did he wear a biker vest with any kind of road name or title?"

"I never got his name and he didn't wear a vest." Shiloh shook her head. "His coloring was orange, though. Orange scales, orange-yellow eyes."

Derric's eyes shifted toward Ruse, who gave a subtle shake of his head. I suspected that description was sadly too broad. Orange was a common coloration among dragons.

"What about the potion?" Ruse asked next. "What would it do for him?"

Shiloh drew in a shaky breath, and I slid my hand into her lap, capturing one of hers.

"It's an extremely volatile, flammable solution called Visakari's Kiss," Shiloh said. "It hasn't been made for centuries, if not longer. It was used in ancient warfare to make huge fireballs."

"Scaly shit wanted a weapon to destroy us all," someone snarled with a pounded fist to the table.

"Why would a dragon need a fuckin' fireball potion?" someone else shot back.

More packmates chimed in, talking over Shiloh who was trying to get a word in to explain more.

From deep within my chest, I released my wolf, lending him my throat, my voice, and all of our shared protective instincts. He growled so loud and furiously that it cut through the noise of my squabbling pack and rattled the table.

"My mate isn't done speaking," I said to the hushed silence that followed. Then I pulled my wolf down, sat back, and massaged Shiloh's nape while waiting for her to continue.

She cleared her throat and squirmed in her seat, her delicious scent blooming and filling my senses. I hid my smile and said nothing, but made a mental note. If putting my packmates in their place turned her on, I'd have to do it more often.

"So, uh, no one alive has seen this happen," she went on. "But it's written in ancient grimoires that a dragon who consumes the potion will breathe fire that is toxic to other dragons. It will have a sedative, numbing effect that knocks them unconscious, eventually killing them by way of systemic organ failure. So not even other dragons are safe from this potion."

The room remained quiet for a long time until Derric said, "So he's trying to rule Shadowburn Cliffs before he takes us."

Ruse made a dismissive noise. "Take out his own people? Hellfire MC, no less?"

"Dragons don't have pack instincts like we do," Derric countered. "Hellfire is the only close-knit community there is. Otherwise, dragons are mostly solitary. They don't have the same sense of loyalty to each other as a species."

"So this guy is trying to become a solo tyrant?" Sawyer

crossed his arms over his chest, still hiding his mark. "Take out Hellfire with this toxic fire potion and rule the territory with fear?"

"That was probably his pipe dream, if the potion is as difficult to make as Shiloh says," Derric said. "He was probably banking on causing panic here in Vargmore. He figured Shiloh would fail at the potion or tell someone what was going on, then set the place on fire."

"To what end, though?" Sawyer asked. "Just to start a war?"

Derric shrugged. "Maybe to look like he's taking initiative? Kissing Hellfire's ass to make a name for himself with them?"

"Our peace agreement benefits them too," Tryn pointed out. "They don't want war any more than we do."

"Respectfully, Alpha," Shiloh piped up. "I don't believe this dragon was scheming that much. He didn't seem... reasonable. He wanted this potion made at all costs, and an absurd amount of it. I don't think he even considered it was nearly impossible to make, despite my telling him multiple times."

"So, are you thinking Sawyer's assessment is the most accurate?" Derric's tone wasn't accusatory, he genuinely wanted to know. That was what made him a good alpha, his willingness to be wrong.

Shiloh nodded. "From what I could tell about him, I think it's the closest guess we have. He's mad for power and not all right in the head. He just wants to be the biggest and baddest... at any cost."

"So he sneaks into enemy territory and threatens one of our citizens," Derric snarled. "He deserves a coward's death, that's for sure." The alpha laid both palms flat on the table. "So, capturing him. Shiloh, you said he'd return at the end of the month?"

"Yes," she said. "He'll come to Stout & Spirit."

"I'll have a team patrol the border around the bar," Sawyer announced. "He's probably coming through vampire territory if no one's spotted him anywhere else."

"I already have a few cameras placed in the trees around the bar," I said. "If Sawyer's team doesn't spot him first, I can keep an eye out from here."

"Great. Get your team out there today, Sawyer, in case our scaly friend decides to show up early. Shiloh?" Derric's expression softened as he looked at my mate. "I don't want you going to the bar or your apartment until we have this dragon under our roof. I assume you're okay to stay here?"

"Um, sure." Shiloh nodded stiffly. "Yes."

"Good. Please let us know if there's anything you need." He nodded at Sawyer. "Get your team together. Everyone else? Be on standby. When the call comes, be ready."

With that final order, everyone stood and began to disperse. I touched Shiloh's shoulder as we rose together. "My room is up the stairs to the left. Third door down. Go on up and make yourself at home. I'll be there in one second, okay?"

"Okay."

Shiloh's voice was flat, her eyes unfocused. The poor little witch had to be exhausted. I bent to kiss her, but she abruptly turned and left. It almost seemed like she had dodged my lips, but she probably just wanted to hurry up and rest. I let her go through the throng of people while I hurried to catch up with Sawyer.

"Enforcer," I called out when I hit the front porch. "Can I get a quick word?"

The other wolf turned slowly, gave me an affirming

nod, and walked around to the side of the lodge for privacy. I followed Sawyer to a place out of sight and earshot, watching his movement as he turned to face me. He leaned against the exterior wall, propping one booted foot up behind him. His hands were shoved into the pockets of his leather jacket, still hiding that dragon's mark. But he otherwise seemed calm, if even relaxed.

"What's on your mind?" he asked.

I considered this wolf more than a packmate. A friend. So I didn't want to come off as confrontational, but I didn't know what else to say besides, "What's up with the dragon mark on your hand?"

"Nothing of your concern," he answered smoothly. So he wasn't even going to deny what it was.

"Are you sure? Because I can't have been the only one who sees the similarities between yours and Shiloh's."

"They look to be the same, true. But I promise you our situations are different."

"Different how?"

"Again, none of your concern."

"Shiloh's in danger," I growled. "The mark was placed upon her as a control tactic. So what does that mean for you? That you *willingly* made a deal with a dragon? Our enemy?"

"Watch it, Orson." Sawyer pushed off the wall, leaning into the air between us. "You're a smart guy, so I know where your brain is going. But the conclusions you're drawing are not accurate. I'm no traitor to the pack, and I don't have to prove that to you again."

"And what if Derric asks you these same questions?"

"I'll tell him the same things I'm telling you. He knows where my loyalty is."

"Really?" I scoffed. "You think the alpha is gonna take

'none of your concern' as a valid answer for a dragon mark on your skin?"

Sawyer crossed his arms, making himself look even bigger. "Listen, Orson. Shiloh is your mate, right?"

"Yes." I couldn't deny the sense of pride, the feeling of rightness making me stand even taller as I answered. "Yes, she's mine."

"And you'd do anything to protect her."

"Of course I would."

Sawyer pulled his hand from his pocket and hovered it in front of my face. The black mark raised the skin on the back of his palm, making a straight line from his middle finger to his wrist. His skin was dry, flaking, and looked painful to the touch.

"I did what I had to to get my mate out of vampire territory," Sawyer said. "Am I proud of it? No. But I made a choice, and this is a consequence. Riley is safe and happy, so would I do it again?" Sawyer dropped his hand and leaned in so close that I could hear the growl emanating from his chest. "I'd make deals with *ten* dragons. Shit, I'd hand myself over to Hellfire MC and get all their fucking marks all over me if that was the price of saving my mate. And Derric understands that."

Sawyer clapped a large hand down on my shoulder when I said nothing in response, the gesture heavy and a touch too aggressive to be merely friendly. Before heading back to his team, he said, "I hope you learn to understand that too, sooner rather than later."

CHAPTER 19

SHILOH

I sat on Orson's bed, replaying parts of the meeting with Howling Death over and over. Especially the part that Orson, my *mate*, had dropped so casually like it was nothing. I still couldn't believe I had heard him correctly. I sat there in his room, which *should* have felt safe and comforting, like I was in a prison cell, trying to rationalize what I'd heard. But no excuse I came up with loosened the knot in my stomach.

And I was fucking tired of trying to excuse bad behavior.

The door opened after a few minutes, my handsome, icy-eyed wolf coming through with a warm, soft expression. "Hey, sorry about that. I just had to talk to Sawyer for a minute."

Right. He was sorry about leaving me here alone for all of five minutes. But not betraying my trust? He didn't even seem aware of what he'd done. Not as he closed the door behind him. Not as he sat next to me on the bed, his arms embracing my stiff body.

"You must be exhausted. You're welcome to sleep as long as you like." Orson kissed my temple. "Or do you want to shower first? The water pressure here is great. You can borrow some of my clothes until we can get stuff from your apartment." Only then did he seem to notice my face and my unresponsive body language and frowned. "Shiloh, is something wrong?"

I sat quietly for a few more seconds, trying to calm the red-hot anger so that I wouldn't scream. "Were you ever planning on telling me that you had cameras in the trees watching my bar?"

Orson's mouth parted in surprise. Then he rubbed his jaw as if choosing his words carefully. "I had honestly forgotten about them until the meeting today," he said quietly.

Trying to keep my cool, I pulled in a long, slow, deep breath. "When did you put them up?"

He took a long time to answer, staring at his shoes. "The morning after you told me to leave the bar."

I nodded, somehow maintaining a calm exterior despite the anger inside me boiling hotter with every word he said. "So right after I explicitly told you that you needed to ask permission before putting cameras in my establishment, you went ahead and set them up outside because...what, you figured you found a loophole? You thought outside cameras would make it okay?"

"Fuck, Shiloh..." Orson started rubbing his forehead.

"No, don't act like *I'm* the unreasonable one here. I ended up letting you install cameras inside because I thought I could trust you. But you never actually needed to do that because you've been watching my place all along!"

"I was going to take down the tree cameras after that,"

he protested. "But then we went on the mountain trip and I just forgot. I'm sorry."

"You're sorry I found out about them, you mean."

"No. I mean, I'm sorry you're upset—"

"How did you expect me to react?" My calm exterior was cracking as I got louder. "If at any point you had just 'fessed up to watching my bar, my *home*, I wouldn't be this upset right now."

"I'm sorry, Shiloh." Orson's head was bent low, staring at the ground. "I fucked up. I'm really sorry."

"You're not, though, so quit saying that." I stood from the bed, physically unable to sit in such close proximity to him. "You're sorry your little secret slipped out and I'm not all just hunky dory with it. You can't just find ways past my boundaries and expect me to take it lying down."

"I know, and I would never do that to you. Not now." Orson lifted his head, his eyes meeting mine with a plea for forgiveness. "I didn't understand back then. But as I've gotten to know you, and started to understand people better in general, I realize what a betrayal that is. I never would have done that had I known what a violation it would be."

Orson stood from the bed and took a few tentative steps toward me but stopped when I backed away. He swallowed, lowering his gaze again. "I want to be a mate you can trust. I would do anything for you, Shiloh. Please tell me how I can fix this."

I shook my head, folding my arms in front of me. "You say you understand and yet you never told me that you had cameras up all along. So my original question stands. Were you *ever* planning on telling me? If the answer is no, then you would have continued lying to me by omission. Do you understand *that?*"

The werewolf remained silent, his eyes growing colder and harder with each passing second.

I didn't want to leave. All signs pointed to Orson being my mate, and even if that weren't a factor, I had started to fall for him. All my life I had fallen easily, too quickly. I'd been swept up by romantic gestures meant to disarm me and good sex that meant nothing. I'd brushed off so many little white lies, plans that were forgotten or canceled, and being treated like a backup plan instead of a priority. Too many times I'd put my own needs aside in the hopes I would be loved in return, eventually.

After Sawyer, I made a promise to myself that I was done with all that. From then on, I would put myself first. I would stop making excuses for shitty behavior. I would stop diminishing myself to keep these men on their comfy pedestals.

So as much as it broke my heart to head toward Orson's door, I did so anyway.

"Where are you going?" he demanded with a snarl.

I paused with my hand on the knob. All I wanted to do was curl up in the safety of that growling chest. But it wasn't really safe. Not when he was keeping things from me and I couldn't trust him.

"Home," I said. "I need some space, so please don't come see me."

"It's not safe for you there."

I could feel the heat of him at my back. The bank of warmth that held me against the cold mountain air now felt volatile. An entity of human emotion mixed with animal instinct.

"You're not the arbiter of my safety, Orson."

I pulled open the door only for his hand to brace against the wood right next to my head and slam it closed.

"Yes, I am." He was standing so close behind me, caging me in, that his breath ruffled my hair. "I am your mate, and it is my sole duty to keep you safe." Orson pushed away from the door, giving me a few feet of space, but it wasn't to let me leave. "And fine. You want me to talk honestly? You're right. I'm not sorry I set up the tree cameras."

I turned around slowly, my back pressed to the door, to find a seething, cornered werewolf staring me down from across the room.

"You really want the truth, Shiloh?" he demanded gruffly, like a challenge. Like I was nowhere near ready for what he was about to tell me.

"That's all I want," I admitted as my heart braced itself for an impact it might never recover from.

"Fine, here it is. My wolf was protective of you from the first moment we scented you. He probably knew you were our mate from the beginning. After you told me to leave, I never would've come back if it wasn't for him. He insisted we protect you. So I put cameras in the trees to appease my wolf. And you know what else?"

"What?"

"I smelled your fear the next morning. And your tears. I knew something had happened. When you came to the lodge to return my money, I smelled it again. I knew you were hiding something, something you were painfully afraid of. So I felt justified in setting those cameras up because you were clearly in need of protecting. But you know what?" He barked out a mirthless laugh. "I still tried to fight it. I tried to explain it away and shove down this pull you had on me. You didn't want me, so what was the point? I didn't remove the cameras, but I stopped watching the footage. Tried to keep you out of sight, out of mind, and all that."

He stopped smiling and returned to staring at me intently. "But now I know. After the time we just spent together, I know you're my mate. And yes, I'm sorry that you're unhappy right now. But I will never be sorry for following my instincts, which have always been to protect you. Even before I knew what you were to me."

"Mate or not, you can't keep me here against my will," I said. "And if we're going to keep being mates, you can't hide things like this from me."

"I will never keep another secret from you again." Orson's head cocked to the side, his gaze menacing. "But if my choice is to barricade you inside this room or risk a deranged dragon finding you, I will absolutely keep you here if I must."

"What if I don't want to be your mate anymore?" The words left me in a rush of anger before I could stop them. And once the question was out there, there was no taking it back. "If what I want doesn't matter, and being your mate is the same thing as being a prisoner, what's the fucking point?"

Orson said nothing for the longest time, his jaw clamping tight with a swallow. "Fate chooses our mates for us. We are meant to be together, driven by forces outside of our control."

"Fate can kiss my ass," I shot back. "I don't want a lying, deceptive prison guard for a mate."

"Shiloh, please." Orson hissed in a breath through his teeth. "I know I'm fucking up and handling this badly. I've never had a mate before, never believed I ever would have one, much less someone as amazing as you." He let out a sigh that deflated his whole chest. "I'm bad when it comes to people, so it stands to reason that I'm a bad mate. But

I'm learning, and I'm trying. The only thing on my mind right now is that you're in danger. Your safety is my first priority. Your happiness is second, I'm sorry. But I'd rather you be alive and angry at me than—" He stopped abruptly, lips thinning as they pressed together. "Than the alternative," he finished off, as though he couldn't even bring himself to say the word *dead* if it pertained to me.

A little bit of my anger faded, though not all of it. Just enough that I moved away from the door. I saw Orson's fists clench, like he was stopping himself from reacting.

"I can understand where you're coming from, although I'm still not happy right now," I said.

"Okay. That's fair," he said with a sharp nod.

"Is there anything else you're keeping from me? Not like your personal stuff, but anything that would piss me off if I knew you weren't telling me."

Orson's jaw clenched, but he ground out the word, "No."

I nodded, shoving the anger away. It wouldn't help if we were both trying to make this work. "After all this is over, you know, assuming Vargmore doesn't become a burning hellscape," I laced my fingers together in front of me, "I think we should take things slow. See how compatible we are as individual people and use that to determine if we're a good match. Instead of just assuming we'll work out because we're fated mates."

"Also fair." He looked at me with a pained expression. "I truly don't want to keep you anywhere against your will, or in any situation you don't want to be in. So if this," he gestured between us, "turns out to be something you don't want, I'll respect that."

Something deep inside me immediately rejected that

notion. Despite how pissed off I was at the moment, every-thing about Orson felt right. He was not the best at expressing himself in human words and gestures, and that was frustrating. But he was trying, like he said. And he did care about me, that much was clear.

Even so, none of that meant he was the right one for me. I wanted to be chosen by who wanted me because I was *me*. Not because some arbitrary force like fate decided we should be together.

So I forced myself to say, "Thank you, Orson. I appreciate you saying that."

He nodded stiffly just as his computer made a pinging sound. "One of the cameras detected motion," he said, heading toward an impressive display of four monitors.

Orson wiggled the mouse and began clicking things. I didn't pay much attention until he said, "Shit," and pulled his phone from his pocket.

"What is it?" I went to look over his shoulder and got an answer immediately.

His middle screen showed a live camera feed. The washed out colors and slightly grainy display pointed directly at Stout & Spirit's front entrance.

A tall figure in a long brown coat stood reading the CLOSED sign and note I'd left on the front door. He turned, and even though the picture quality wasn't the best, I recognized his cruel face. His slitted pupils. And the orange scales running up his neck to his cheek.

"That's him." I pointed a shaky finger at the screen. "The one who wanted the potion. It's him."

"Derric, the dragon's at the bar right now," Orson barked into the phone. "Shiloh just ID'd him. Get Sawyer and his—what? Yes, Alpha." He ended the call without another word. "All of Howling Death is riding out."

"I'm coming too." He was already heading for the door, and I hurried to stay on his heels.

"No, you're staying here." Orson whipped around, blocking the exit.

"Like fuck I am. It's my business, my *home*, Orson."

"What did we just argue about?" the werewolf snarled. "You are his target, Shiloh. I'm not putting you at risk."

"What risk is there with all of Howling Death coming to confront him?" I demanded. "You said yourself that he was too much of a coward to take the pack on himself." I took hold of Orson's forearm. "Please. I just need to be there when you guys take him down." A smile pulled at my lips despite the severity of the situation. "My mate will keep me safe, won't you?"

He made a sound somewhere between a growl and a purr. "I'll rip his fucking head off with my bare teeth."

Okay, I couldn't lie. It was damn hot that he was *that* protective of me.

"And you'd deny letting me watch?" I implored. "We can celebrate right after you slay that monster for me."

The forearm I'd been holding snaked around my waist, drawing me in close. "Does this mean you're no longer mad at me?"

"Don't make me stay back here and I'll definitely be a lot less mad."

"Ugh, fine," Orson grunted. "But you're staying on my bike, far away from him."

"Deal."

My hand slipped into his and we joined the pack of werewolves streaming out of the lodge to their motorcycles parked outside. Everyone was hard-faced and snarling, snapping their jaws as they mounted their steeds, the animal side eager to take down an enemy as a single unit.

I held onto my werewolf as I climbed on behind him, his torso rumbling under my hands just as much as the bike was.

We weren't perfect but he was mine.

And he was about to slay a dragon for me.

CHAPTER 20

ORSON

Howling Death was just as coordinated and in-tune with each other as a motorcycle club as we were a wolf pack. On two wheels, we hit the same formation as we would have on four paws, fanning out in an arrow shape behind our alpha in the lead.

I was squarely in the middle, the ideal place to be with my precious cargo in the seat behind me. Shiloh held on to me loosely as we rode toward her bar, not the tight embrace she had me in when we returned from the mountain. She held onto my waist in order to not fly off the bike and nothing more. The touch felt cold, and I already missed how things were before. Her head on the back of my shoulder and the squeeze of her arms, her fingers stroking over my chest.

Once we were rid of this dragon, I hoped I hadn't fucked things up beyond repair. Fate, the moon, whatever forces of nature controlled our destiny, for some reason, chose to give me the gift of a mate. And I was on the verge of losing her before we'd truly begun.

My packmates ahead were slowing, their brake lights coming to life like a monster with six red eyes. I saw the yellow porch light of Stout & Spirit illuminating the front facade of the building and the tall figure pacing back and forth in the gravel driveway.

The figure abruptly stopped his pacing and turned to face us. I braked so hard, my bike jolted and my tires skidded on the road. I hadn't taken a close look at his facial features on the camera feed, but they were unmistakable now.

I fucking knew this dragon.

He recognized me in the same instant, a slow, menacing smile spreading across his face. Derric, Ruse, Sawyer, and the other front-liners of the pack surrounded the dragon shifter, but he didn't seem to take notice. The ugly bastard remained singularly focused on me.

Derric let out a short, sharp whistle, a signal for us to get ready to shift, which also caught the dragon's attention. The reptile broke eye contact with me to meet the alpha's gaze with a relaxed unhurriedness. Like we were the ones inconveniencing him.

"All of Howling Death come to see me? What an honor," the dragon drawled.

"I suggest you stop talking," Derric barked.

The dragon made a show of zipping his lips with his long, black claws. My wolf's hackles rose, personally insulted by the arrogance of this male.

"Normally, I'd give you one chance to return to your own territory, provided that you never set foot in Vargmore again," the alpha said. "But from what I understand, this is at least your third time trespassing into our home. The first two times, you threatened and injured one of our civilians. Is that not correct?"

"Ahhh." The dragon rolled his orange eyes toward me again, settling over my shoulder. "The little witch went off and tattled after all. Such a shame. I thought she was one to honor agreements."

My fist squeezed so hard, it rolled the throttle and pulled a roar from my engine. "You don't say a word about her," I growled. "You don't even look at her."

The dragon clicked his tongue, amused. "Protective are we, Orson?" He folded his arms in front of him, grinning widely. "Did my deal with the witch conjure up a little romance? How lucky for you."

"Don't say my name. You don't know me." My wolf was moments away from leaping out of my skin, ready to jump over the handlebars and all the wolves and bikes ahead of me to get at this reptilian pest.

"Typical half-breed. Always rewriting history to whichever side suits you." The dragon placed his hands on his hips and looked around. "Does your wolf pack know? How about your little witch?"

"Know what?" Shiloh whispered behind me.

"Nothing," I bit out.

"Why did he call you a half-breed?" she pressed. "Is that even..."

"Oh, it's more than possible. It happened all the time before the species of Shyftworld separated themselves into neat little territories." The dragon grinned, smug and satisfied at his captive audience. "Orson never told you all he was born in Shadowburn Cliffs? Spent the early years of his life there. He would've stayed if only he had sprouted wings and scales instead of fur and paws."

"So what?" I shouted, feeling like my chest was being crushed while grabbing desperately for a handhold on the edge of a cliff. "I'm a wolf, not a dragon. I'm nothing like you."

"Ah, but you've still got some dragon in you. Ever look in the mirror?" He pointed his two forefingers at his own eyes; bright, fiery orange with slitted pupils. "Those are the eyes of the ice dragons, our ancestors. No matter how much you try to deny your own heritage, Orson, you know for a fact that no werewolf has ever sported peepers like yours."

My teeth ground so hard, I was certain I would break my own jaw. "I'm no. Fucking. Dragon."

He sighed, shoulders drooping like he pitied me. "I can see why you believed that. Especially with how our father kicked you to the curb the moment you displayed wolf traits. How he always favored me as the golden child over you."

Shiloh's hands jerked in her hold on my waist. "Did he say *our...?*"

"Yes, my dear. An astute observation." The dragon's eyes lit up as they landed on her again. "Orson and I are brothers."

"Half-brothers," I corrected. "Because *your* father decided to abuse a she-wolf."

"Eh, semantics. You and I are still family."

"We are not!" I snarled.

"Enough of this!" Derric raised a hand in the air. "None of this backstory fucking matters—"

"Actually, it does," the dragon interrupted. "This is very important for you to hear, Alpha. You might want to think twice about letting half-breeds into your pack." He paused just long enough for me to wonder what he was getting at. "It was actually my dear brother's idea to make the witch do some magic for us."

"What?" Shiloh whispered the word but it was a roar in my ears. Her hands pulled away from my waist, and that small motion felt like our last tenuous connection had been severed.

"Don't believe his lies. You know you can't trust him." I hated to sound so damn desperate, even though I was.

"I'm not lying!" Again with that snakelike grin. "How would Orson know where to find the silver deadnettle if he didn't have eyes in the sky?"

Oh, this sneaky fucker. He saw the distance between Shiloh and I, then proceeded to wedge his way in there until the gap was as wide as a canyon. With her trust in me so freshly shaken, it wouldn't take much to put even more doubts in her mind.

Who knew how much he saw through that mark he left on her? Or because he'd been stalking us through the mountains.

"Because I lived in those woods!" I cried out. "And I have a nose like a wolf because I *am* one."

"And you're so desperate to impress a mate, you'd even turn to a dragon, your enemy, if it would benefit us both."

"Shut the fuck up!" I snarled. "I would never."

But the damage had already been done. I could sense the change in the air, scent my half brother's smugness all too clearly.

"I'm done listening to this," the alpha bit out. "You, dragon, are an active threat to *my* territory and its citizens." Derric lifted up from his seat, standing on his foot pegs as gray fur rippled over his body. "We'll return your corpse as a message to those in Shadowburn Cliffs. Howling Death!"

The pack answered his bellowed call, tearing off their clothing as men became wolves. I joined them, fighting my way to the front. The secrets of my past I had intended to bury and leave behind would have to be addressed later. Maybe I would no longer have a pack as well as a mate after this was done. But no matter. My last act as a Howling Death wolf would be fighting alongside my packmates, protecting the territory and my mate.

No matter what she thought of me from now on, I would always consider her mine.

Howling Death rushed the dragon as a single mass of snarls and snapping jaws. We surrounded him, but the coward used his one advantage—flight.

Broad orange-gold wings sprouted from his back, lifting him into the air. I didn't intend to let that stop me, so I jumped onto a packmate's back and lunged at the enemy. It didn't matter if I shared blood with him, he harmed my mate. Whatever his plans with the potion and territory were irrelevant to me in that moment. His blood needed to spill for what he did to Shiloh.

I was airborne for a second, maybe two, when something broad and heavy like a tree trunk slammed into my ribs. The ground caught me hard, knocking out the rest of what little air I had left.

The dragon finished shifting in midair while I wheezed for a breath on the ground, his tail thrashing around in case other wolves got the idea to jump at him. He stretched his long, scaly neck forward, letting out a keening cry. Then, with another beat of wings, he lifted well out of our reach and began flying away.

Some wolves ran, following him from the ground, but the dragon was already climbing higher until he was no longer visible through the clouds.

"Fucking knew that would happen," Derric's voice said

from somewhere nearby, which meant he'd already shifted back. "You okay, Orson?"

A whine left my wolf's throat, my ears flattened and tail low with the shame of what had just been revealed.

"It's alright." Derric scratched my scruff. "I'll take your word over his any day of the week. We'll regroup and find a way to take him down."

I pulled back my wolf until I was sitting naked on the ground. Derric's hand rested on my shoulder while I stared at my feet. "Thank you, Alpha."

He patted my shoulder before standing. "Looks like you should talk to your mate, though."

I tried to collect myself before rising to my feet and finding my clothes. Everyone else was doing the same, commiserating about the dragon getting away as they got dressed and remounted their motorcycles.

Derric let out another whistle through his teeth. "We regroup at the lodge and make another plan." To me, he said, "Join us when you're ready."

I nodded, and there was no time left to stall as motorcycles took off, leaving me, my bike, and the beautiful witch standing next to it.

"So, it's true?" Shiloh asked, her tone taking on that deceptive calm while the scent of anger and hurt flared. "All of it?"

I swallowed, struggling to take a deep breath. "It's true that Mokir and I are half brothers—"

"Oh, so you *are* on a first-name basis."

"No, it's not..." I started coughing, my lungs still aching from being hit by the dragon's tail. "I swear to you I haven't seen him in decades. I hate him. We're not friends, and I absolutely was not in on his plan. Please believe me, Shiloh."

"I want to, Orson. I really wish I could." Her eyes glittered with unshed tears, lower lip wobbling. "But you lied *again*. I asked you not even an hour ago if there was anything else you were keeping from me. And this? The fact that you lied about having a dragon *brother* is worse than I could have imagined. How could you? After what I told you about my mother--"

I closed my eyes as she choked up, trying to force another painful breath into my lungs. "I'm so sorry, it didn't feel right to explain it all right then. I...I don't know what else to say."

"Probably better if you don't say anything." She sniffed and stuffed her hands in the pockets of her sweater. "I can't go back to the lodge with you."

Fear sliced through me like claws, my brain grabbing onto her words and reading into what she didn't say. "You have to, it's not safe anywhere else. You don't have to stay with me, but—"

"I can stay with the witch community. But I can't be around you." She sniffed again and released a deep sigh. "I need some space to clear my head."

She wasn't being explicit, but she didn't need to be. I knew she was ending it. Leaving me.

I had no chance of winning her smiles and laughter again, not with the chasm between us. Not with this detachment she now held herself with.

"I need to know you won't try to come find me," Shiloh went on. "You won't reach out or show up where I'm staying. When I'm ready, I'll reach out to you."

There it was, the final nail in the coffin. If I agreed, I would be giving up the clever witch I'd fallen in love with, my mate. If I didn't, I was a selfish asshole she'd hate even more.

In the end, my instinct to please her, to give her everything she wanted, won out. I may have been both man and beast, but she owned all parts of me.

Through an impossibly tight throat I said, "I will do as you ask and leave you be."

CHAPTER 21

ORSON

Tryn's hands moved in front of his face like he was gathering up strings, his eyes not focusing on me but somewhere far away. He pinched his thumb and forefinger of each hand and drew them apart, as if stretching out invisible lengths of string between them. The rest of the pack waited with bated breath as Tryn inspected the air between his hands.

"Orson tells the truth. He did not conspire with the dragon," he announced. "His truth thread is perfectly intact. No knots or kinks to be seen."

My chest eased, letting out the breath that I felt like I'd been holding for hours. Still, an ache had settled there ever since Shiloh told me not to contact her. I had a feeling many moons would pass before I felt any relief in the pit of my chest.

"Good," Derric said from his place at the far end of the great room. "I had no doubts, but for anyone that did, let this be your proof." The alpha leaned forward, his sharp eyes scanning the room. "Orson is one of us, a Howling

Death wolf. The circumstances of his birth does not make him an enemy. The one we're fighting is an enemy we've always known, a scaly bastard with wings. And we'll drag him out of the fucking sky if we have to." Derric slouched in his seat, awaiting any complaints or grumbles. When none came, he looked at me. "Now that I've squashed any conspiracy theories before they can arise, is there anything you can tell us about this dragon, Orson?"

With everything churning through me at that moment, I was grateful he did not refer to Mokir as my brother or even half brother. I might have done something I'd regret, like snap my jaws or growl at my alpha.

"I haven't seen him since I was teenager, when I was forced out of Shadowburn Cliffs," I said. "Of what little I do know, I'm not sure how much is useful."

"Is he or your—*his* father, associated with Hellfire MC, to your knowledge?"

"I believe our father may have been exiled from Hellfire. I remember him being very...bitter and hateful toward the club. Especially Aran, the president." My eyes lifted toward Derric. "Our original theory probably has merit. I think Mokir wanted to drink the potion from Shiloh—" my chest squeezed painfully at the mention of her name "—so that his toxic fire would wipe out Hellfire, giving him an opportunity to seize power over the dragons. And after that, us."

"And now that he's been discovered by us, any ideas on what his next move is?"

I shook my head. "I don't know. He flew away when confronted. He...he may try to take hostages? I truly don't know his thought process."

"We should have civilians go into hiding," Ruse suggested. "Bunker underground, ideally. Especially the witches, just in case he's still intent on getting this potion made."

"I agree," Sawyer cut in. "Everyone should go underground. I wouldn't put it past him to start fires indiscriminately."

"Orson." Derric leaned toward me. "Can you put out an alert that everyone in the territory will see?"

"I can push a notification to every phone in the territory, yes."

"Good, do that. Everyone else, spread out and start searching the higher elevations. Dragons can't stay in the sky forever. He will need to land in order to eat and rest."

"He'll avoid the colder regions," I said. "If his blood temperature drops too much, he'll slow down and get all sluggish. So he won't be too far from us."

"Where there's smoke, there's fire," Ruse quipped before clapping his hands once. "Let's go, Howling Death."

The pack filed out of the lodge with a commotion of howls, barks, and growls while I headed up to my room. To send an alert to everyone in the territory, I needed to access the emergency system I set up years ago on my computer for situations precisely like this one.

It was the work of a moment to push the notification out, and I was out of my chair the moment I hit send. Maybe I should have expected Tryn to darken my doorway, but I nearly crashed headfirst into him on my way out.

"Tryn, what?" I barked. "We gotta move."

"Don't rush into this like a martyr, Orson." He had that faraway look in his eyes again, like he was watching something play out in the distance. "It's not too late yet."

"What, do you read minds now?" I snapped. "I'm joining the hunting party with everyone else."

"No, you're not." Now the other wolf's eyes focused on me, his expression knowing. "That was clever what you did, making sure no one would search the colder regions. How do you know your half-brother will be there?"

"Stay out of this, prophet," I growled. "Nobody touches that dragon but me."

"You can't take on a dragon by yourself and win," he argued. "Shiloh won't be impressed by your burnt-up corpse. Quit being an idiot, and let your pack back you up."

"My mate deserves justice even if she's done with me." I got up close and personal to my packmate's face. Tryn and I were pretty evenly matched if it came to a scuffle, but I had the advantage of vengeance burning through me. "Get out of my way, and let me do this one last thing for her."

"You know I saw your mate thread while I was finding your truth thread. Want to know what it looked like?"

I hesitated for too long but resisted the carrot he dangled in my face. "It doesn't matter. I'm not right for her."

"It was strong, bright. No frayed bits or knots in it. It looked damn near unbreakable. I've seen mate threads that look as thin as hairs, just waiting for that straw on the camel's back to break it."

"Well, rest assured. That will be ours soon."

"For fucking moon's sake, Orson! It doesn't have to be." Tryn's frustration was palpable, but that was nothing new. "Your connection with your mate has to be tended to, cared for and nurtured. It's not too late to save it, but if this fucking dragon kills you, it will be." The prophetic wolf leaned back, folding his arms across his chest. "Do you want Shiloh to mourn you for the rest of her life?"

"She won't mourn me," I said. "At least not for long."

"She does want you, even if she's hurt and confused. This suicide mission is not the way to go."

"Fucking shit, Tryn! How come you don't have a mate if you know so damn much?"

He only seemed amused by my outburst, stroking his beard with a chuckle. "It turns out, I can't see my own fate threads. Everyone else is fair game, but when it comes to myself, I guess the moon decided I'd best be left in the dark."

It wasn't lost on me what a burden that must be, to see everyone's fate except your own. But in any case, it wasn't my business. Not my concern. Tryn was trying to look out for me as a brother would, but even if he could see my fate, he didn't walk in my paws. He hadn't lived my life, couldn't know this bloodthirst on my tongue that would only be satisfied by half brother's death.

"I hope fate is kind to you, Tryn," I said. "I hope the moon's light shows your path and leads you to your destiny. Now please get out of my way, because this is mine."

My packmate's lip curled and he didn't budge. "I have half a mind to throw you in a damn kennel like a human's pet."

"I don't want to fight, but if you do, there'll be blood on your muzzle."

"I know. You see me wrasslin' you?"

Tryn spread his arms, staying in place. I shoved past him, and the only resistance he gave was his body weight.

"You have the right to make your own choices, Orson," he called, still facing the inside of my room as I went for the stairs. "I wish you would trust that this is a wrong one."

I hesitated on the middle landing. "I know it is."

"Then why do it?"

I shook my head and continued my way down. "Because doing the wrong thing is all I'm good at."

))) ❭ ❭ ◗ ● ◖ ❬ ❬ (((

ONCE OUTSIDE THE LODGE, I stripped off my clothes and shifted. I took a moment to check out the scent trails of my packmates that had dispersed throughout the territory, then picked one heading north to follow. This way, it wouldn't— at first— seem like I'd gone rogue. By the time they figure it out, hopefully the deed would be done.

A few miles later, the trail took a left, rounding the foothills at the base of our mountain range. I kept heading north, climbing the first rise in elevation like a human running up an escalator.

This was a different route than Shiloh and I had taken on my bike, but it would lead to the same peak. I couldn't pinpoint the instinct, couldn't locate the how or why I knew Mokir would be there, but my certainty was absolute.

It was like following a scent trail but not exactly. Something deep and instinctual that I'd never felt before guided me. I had never even been aware of it before today, before Mokir said I had some dragon inside me.

Sawyer and Fallon said their mates believed themselves to be human until their latent wolves woke up in the presence of others of our kind. Could it be the same for me when it came to my dragon half?

I was the only hybrid shifter I knew of, and no one seemed to have the answers. Not the ancient wisdom of the feral pack who took me in, nor the modern Howling Death, or the witches with their wealth of magic and history. I never belonged anywhere because I was the only one of my kind.

I had only ever felt like I had belonged with Shiloh, and now that was destroyed. Even if she came to the conclusion that Mokir had been lying, could she really trust me again, knowing what I was? Her mother had betrayed the wolves of Vargmore for helping the dragons, for fuck's sake. Shiloh had been trying to get away from that shameful association all her life. And then to have me as a mate? She was smarter than that. Better than that.

I felt like a fake wolf, even though it was still the only animal I felt living under my human skin. Even now, despite this new intuition guiding me to my half-brother, no new awareness prowled inside me. I didn't feel like I could grow wings or breathe fire. Like always, it was just me and my silver-furred animal.

My wolf had been quiet for a while. He was steadfast, determined. He fully supported this new guiding instinct leading us to Mokir and didn't give a huff where it came from. He wanted vengeance for our mate, to end the danger present to her. The delusional furball still believed she would want us, accept and approve of us as her mate after all this.

The rational, human side of me knew it was over and that it would remain the biggest regret of my life. Once Derric figured out I intentionally led the pack away from Mokir's trail, I might also get exiled out of Howling Death.

If I lived through this.

I hiked onward, my four paws never stopping even as the sun fell and the moon rose. Only right before the sun rose again did I allow myself to rest for a drink of water in an icy stream. Once refreshed, I hunted a small meal for the strength to keep going. Despite the presence of pheasants around, I bypassed them for a young male hare. Too many memories with pheasants.

The cold air penetrated my fur at this elevation, and my paw pads ached with soreness when I finally caught his scent. Burnt wood and debris clogged my senses, like I'd happened upon a forest fire. But the landscape was pristine—untouched wilderness with snow-capped peaks in the distance. The stench was horrid, but I pressed on, knowing I was nearing my ultimate goal.

Mokir was close enough to be seen. If he wanted to be seen, that was.

I scanned the trees in the small clearing I'd found myself in, looking for any conspicuous reptilian shapes in the pine boughs. My shitty canine vision didn't reveal much, though. I'd see better if I was human, but that would leave me vulnerable.

"So you figured it out, little brother."

I whipped around to find Mokir sauntering toward me, naked in his human form except for the orange scales shimmering across his skin in different areas. Dragons liked to do that, I didn't know why. It wasn't like werewolves walked around on two legs with canine ears or fur on our faces.

I shifted to human to respond to him. "What are you talking about?"

"You tapped into that dragon instinct to find me." He grinned with a mouth full of fangs. "Always knew you had it in you, despite your genetics choosing the inferior animal."

I ignored his jabs, as I'd always done since childhood. "Why did you really come here? Why harass my mate?"

"Because I was bored."

"Bored? You crossed into enemy territory and left your mark on an innocent witch because you're *bored?*"

"Yeah," the dragon replied with a shrug. "Nothing's happening in Shadowburn Cliffs. All we do is mine and process draitrium to sell to the vampires so they can day walk. Business is down because Thorne doesn't want a territory full of sun-junkies. Aran doesn't have an ambitious scale on his body, so Hellfire MC isn't doing shit about it. No new business ventures, territory expansion, nothing. Shadowburn is as stagnant as a puddle, and if something doesn't change, it's going to dry up."

"So that's what this is?" "I growled. "You harm a witch and make threats against the territory to shake things up? To get Aran's attention?"

"Nah, fuck him. Dragons need a new leader, and Aran is too soft. Rumor has it he even made a deal with one of you wolfkind."

I thought back to the mark on Sawyer's hand and his defensiveness over it, but then a bigger realization dawned on me. "You really are trying to overthrow Hellfire," I said in disbelief. "The pack thought it might be true, but you really are unhinged enough to betray your own kind."

"Unhinged?" Mokir scoffed. "Try 'revolutionary'. I'm leading dragonkind into a new age. One where tyrants don't consort with the enemy and ignore everyone from their thrones."

I barked out a laugh. "How do you expect to do that? One dragon against a horde of them. You don't even have your toxic fire potion now."

"Easy. I'll double the size of our territory by burning Vargmore until it's nothing but a husk." More scales appeared on his skin as wide, reptilian wings spread from his back. "Starting with you, little brother."

He lifted into the air with one powerful beat of his wings, his features shifting away from human to the fire-breathing monster within him.

I turned and started running, but I wasn't fast enough to escape the heat already singing my back.

CHAPTER 22
ORSON

I took a running leap, somehow shifted in the middle of a freefall, and landed on all fours just as the stream of fire lit up the air where I had been a moment before. Diving into a cluster of bushes, I realized my error when I noticed how dry the branches were. Flames engulfed me and I ran out, charging so hard through the wall of fire that I didn't notice the burrs and thorns scraping me.

All I could do was run. While I'd been at the top of the food chain, an apex predator all my life, there was little difference between me and a rabbit now. I was this dragon's fucking prey. Not only that, he was toying with me and having the time of his life.

No matter how fast I ran, I could hear the beat of his wings and feel the great gusts of air. The sounds of his wings were slow as he followed me at a leisurely pace. Sometimes he blasted fire at my heels, spurring me into a harder sprint. Other times, he blew it over my head, creating a fire wall in front that forced me to stop and change directions abruptly.

The infernal beast anticipated every fake-out and dodge I made. How could he not with his bird's-eye view? His roars sounded like laughter. He was enjoying this, while I was quickly running out of gas.

There had to be a way. Maybe not if I fought him head-to-head, but I had to buy time. Had to outsmart him somehow. Lizards were not known for their strategic thinking, after all.

Another blast of fire lit my fur and I rolled with a yelp to put it out. I hadn't even gotten my feet under me when he aimed a second blast at the ground. With a desperate scramble to my four paws, I ran in the only clear direction I saw—straight toward the dragon.

I ran between his front legs, keeping low to the ground when an idea struck me. I lifted my snout and made the decision in an instant. Flipping to my back again, I opened my jaws as wide as I could and sank my teeth into Mokir's soft, undefended belly.

The dragon let out a bellow of pain, and everything spun as he scrambled to get me off. Not only did I clamp down harder, I got my paws into the action, kicking and clawing at the dragon's belly. The scent of blood assaulted my nose and the hot, metallic liquid was filling my mouth, but I refused to let go.

I upped the ante, wrenching my head back and forth with all my strength to tear into him deeper, to make the gaping wound bigger. When he finally managed to tear me away, I took a big ol' mouthful with me.

The dragon's roar filled my ears, and then I was flying through the air. *Fuck, this is gonna hurt.*

How right I was. It felt like a battering ram had slammed into my neck and shoulder. My vision went blurry, and the impact forced me to drop the chunk of dragon flesh from my mouth.

I must have truly blacked out for a second because the next thing I knew, a massive orange dragon was stampeding straight toward me. Mokir's long neck stretched out in a straight line, his spiked head the weapon that would surely end me. Those glowing orange eyes were no longer playful but dead-set on murder.

His head pulled back, neck forming an S-shape as I fought to get my feet under me. In the next moment, the dragon lunged forward and I was surrounded by fire.

The heat was suffocating, like walls pressing in on all sides. I didn't know how I moved. I might have rolled or just stumbled out of the path of the fire, but my next breath was fresh, albeit hot, air and the heat was only uncomfortable rather than blistering pain.

Risking a glance over my shoulder, I saw that Mokir had set a giant redwood tree on fire. That must have been what he threw me at after ripping me off of his belly.

The dragon was injured and therefore pissed. He clutched one scaled, clawed hand to the wound on his belly as he came after me, slower now, but not because he was playing. Smoke curled out of his nostrils and the corners of his gasping mouth. Mokir seemed to be huffing, almost wheezing. He pulled in deep breaths and only blew out smoke and embers on the exhales. Where was the fire?

I started running again and he kept after me, monstrous and nightmarish with his three legs limping along the forest floor. We were under the cover of trees now, so maybe he didn't want to risk getting whacked by branches in his belly if he took flight.

His wings, I realized. *Hurt his wings and he'll stay grounded.*

Mokir's neck rolled back before he lunged forward with another earth-shattering roar. I braced myself for the wall of heat, though none came. Just more smoke with a few sparks and embers. The dragon pounded one massive fist against the ground, clearly frustrated.

It dawned on me then, a lightbulb moment that felt like clouds parting for sunlight during a storm.

Dragons could run out of fuel.

I almost let out a howl of victory but kept my jaws clamped shut. Better if Mokir didn't catch on that I knew his little secret. Making those wings unflyable was still top priority. Besides, I had no idea how long dragons need to refuel their lungs or whatever. Minutes? Hours? He kept trying, so I had a feeling it wouldn't be long.

Staying low to the ground, I slunk in a wide circle around the dragon, taking cover in some dense shrubs. That turned out to be a mistake for a reason other than fire.

Something as big as a tree trunk slammed down behind me. Then it lifted and did the same thing in front of me. Trying to get out of a path I couldn't predict, the thing slammed down on the base of my spine, which sent shooting pain up my body and made my back end go limp.

Fucking moon. I had been so preoccupied with the fire and wings that I didn't stop to account for the dragon's fucking *tail.*

The next tail slam came down and I rolled out of the way, saving my own hide by mere inches. My own tail and back legs were ringing with agony, but at least I could still feel them. Coming to my feet, I wasted no time charging at the webbing of the monster's wing—the skin stretched between the wing's bones.

All I could reach was a lower portion of the wing, so I made it count. The webbing was surprisingly easy to tear with my teeth and claws. Thicker than his belly but it bled readily.

A scream pierced my ears before I was torn off and sent flying again. I closed my eyes, bracing for impact. Another crash with a tree just might end me, but no. I hit the ground and slid for a few feet. I was back in the clearing where we'd started.

Mokir started after me, crashing through the treeline like a dinosaur from a prehistoric forest. This time, I knew I couldn't wait for him to come up on me. Gasping for breath from the impact, I got to my feet and ran straight to him.

He pulled up short, apparently startled that I'd meet him head on, which was what I'd been hoping for. The dragon reared back, made that S-shape with his neck again, and I went for the exposed areas, jaws first.

I aimed for his chest at the base of his neck. Because of the angle and his protective scales, the bite was shallow. But it still bled. I didn't know dragon anatomy, but with any luck, I was near a major artery.

Unable to grasp and hold on, I dropped to the ground and immediately lunged between his front legs. Now that he knew what I was doing, Mokir reared up, but I followed.

Pushing all the strength I had left into my back legs, I jumped and latched onto another soft area of dragon belly. He wrenched me off with a deafening roar, sending me on another flying journey.

This landing really knocked the wind out of me, despite rolling to soften the impact. Not to mention my sides had felt like knives plunged into me with every breath for a while. I was covered in burns and probably had nerve damage in my tail and back legs. I could only keep making him bleed for so much longer. I had two, maybe three more instances of being thrown around like a ragdoll left in me, but after that?

I felt like a half-dead mouse getting batted around by a cat.

This is why wolves run in packs, I thought, returning shakily to my feet.

Another voice, one I recognized as my wolf's, growled in reply. *Why do you need a pack? Are you not strong enough to do right by your mate?*

My head swam with fuzzy images, memories that all blended together. All of Shiloh. When she first confronted me with that baseball bat over her shoulder. Her hands reaching out toward my wolf, her scent and voice filling him with calm and ease. Her flushed face and the heaves of her chest when she'd needed me during the full moon. The taste of her then and afterwards. Our times together here, in these woods. Not just the sex we had but the conversations and laughter.

No, this fight wasn't meant to have a pack involved. This was about her, my mate. No one could fight this dragon *but* me. Because he had threatened, had *harmed*, the most important person in my life.

Bleeding from at least three places, Mokir eyed me warily as I rose to all fours to confront him again. He still had the advantage but knew he couldn't be careless. Plumes of smoke curled from his nostrils while his lips pulled back in a terrifying grin. Panic stabbed at my chest, and I tried to discreetly sniff at the air. Did he...?

The dragon reared back with a great gulp of breath. The air between us distorted, and I could already feel the oppressive heat. I turned and started running, darting behind a boulder that was immediately engulfed in flames.

My flank that had touched the rock burned with a hot, stinging pain that made me howl, and I ran for cover.

Yeah, the fucking dragon had his fire back.

I was so preoccupied with escaping the fire that I again didn't anticipate the tail.

It barreled into my side, shoving me into another rock. This time, I heard the distinct pop of a bone breaking and felt the radiating pain that followed.

The tail pulled away, and now I was limping on three legs, just trying to get anywhere that wasn't fire and pain. My broken leg slowed me way down though, and I screamed in agony as a blast of fire hit me directly. I could smell my own flesh cooking, hear the sizzle and pop of burning tissue and fat.

I wasn't going to win this. I could only drag my burnt, battered body so far. A few flesh wounds on him compared to my getting absolutely wrecked? It was no contest. Only shock and adrenaline kept me going, kept me limping and dragging myself away like the prey I was.

The blistering heat was being replaced by a deep sense of cold, and I knew my body was shutting down. My nervous system could no longer process all the pain signals, could no longer support my racing heart and aching lungs.

I had failed not only my mate but the territory.

I was getting so fucking cold that I began to see my own breath puffing in front of me.

Mokir had given me a bit of a head start, but he was on me again in no time. A light shove knocked me over, and I hit the ground to see him towering over me, grinning once again.

I was so damn cold that my whole body shivered now. He probably wouldn't even finish me off, he could just watch the life drain out of me instead.

I'm so sorry, Shiloh.

Pressure built up in my stomach and chest. Weirdly, that sensation was freezing cold too, like my insides were turning to solid blocks of ice. If that wasn't a sign of dying, I didn't know what was.

The pressure inside me mounted as Mokir shoved me again, rolling me to my back. My stomach began to convulse, and I felt the urge to cough. Knowing how painful it would be on my likely-broken ribs, I suppressed the urge. Although projectile vomiting as my final act on the monster who was about to kill me would be funny. Shiloh would probably laugh.

The dragon stood directly over me now. With my vision going out, I could only make out the rough shapes of his body—front legs on either side of me, long neck, triangular head.

Another icy convulsion rolled up from my stomach to my throat, the urge to throw up stronger this time. My flagging strength made it harder to keep my jaws clamped shut.

Mokir reared his back, his jaws open and relaxed enough that I could see the glow of the fireball inside his mouth. He paused with his neck curled back, the size and brightness of that fireball growing.

More ice, more pressure building up in my stomach and throat. I knew I wouldn't be able to stop it this time. *Oh well. Puking on a dragon as a last hurrah it is. At least the pack will have stories to tell, if they ever find me.*

My upper body rolled forward with a strength I didn't know I had. The convulsion started low in my belly and rippled upward like an icy wave. I opened my mouth just as the dragon opened his.

Fire singed the fur on my ears and top of my head. The

pain was a bygone thought as a horrific shrieking sound pierced my ears. The fuzzy outline of the dragon was now thrashing back and forth, the high-pitch sound full of horror and agony.

It took me too long to realize with a detached fascination that it was not vomit pouring out of my mouth.

It was ice.

CHAPTER 23

SHILOH

The emergency alert had hit everyone's phones three days ago. I knew it had to be Orson's system, had to have been him who crafted the message for everyone to bunker underground until further instruction.

On our second day of hiding, the mark on my arm disappeared. I nearly cried with relief, thinking this nightmare was finally over. Surely this meant the dragon was dead. Or had at least been captured and agreed to release me from its hold. I waited by my phone and as it continued to stay silent, all of my optimism drained away just like its battery.

I watched my phone until the battery died, checking the messages constantly for an update from Howling Death, or better yet, a personal message from Orson himself. The reception in the bunker under the human lodge was shoddy at best, but I clung stubbornly to that hope like a lifeline. Like the idiot I was.

Why should I expect to hear from him after what I accused him of? My trust had already been shaky because of what I had just found out about the cameras, and I reacted with those emotions after confronting the dragon. After more time to think and calm down, I realized how nonsensical it was to believe the dragon over him. Especially if Howling Death had no cause for concern.

I still couldn't wrap my head around the fact that Orson was half dragon shifter at all, but that wasn't his fault, was it? He couldn't help the circumstances he was born into.

And yet...how could it happen? A werewolf with a dragon. The two species had been separated, sequestered by their respective territories for the better part of a century. There had likely been a kidnapping of some kind. Some poor she-wolf had been taken from her pack, her family, and put into a hellish situation she most likely did not consent to.

The strange part was that I'd never heard such a story. We had plenty of legends about wolves being taken by vampires back when that conflict was at its peak. Werewolf blood was supposedly especially addictive to vampires. Before the territories were established, pups were stolen from their homes to be kept as blood pets. So their parents retaliated by killing vampires. This angered the vampires, who responded by kidnapping more wolves for their blood, and on and on it went until a tentative peace agreement was reached and the four territories established.

But dragons had no thirst for blood, so why would they kidnap a werewolf?

Maybe there was no clear why. The answer might have been simple as someone just choosing to walk up to my bar and forcing me into creating a destructive potion for them. Some unhinged psycho and their random unlucky victim. Although it wouldn't have been so random if the dragon had to go into enemy territory to find said victim. Which suggested that the encounter could have been consensual.

My gut instantly rejected that notion. After the dragons backed the vampires, supplying them with their daywalking drugs as they were murdering werewolves? There was no fucking way. After my mother was publicly shamed and ousted for letting dragons escape to the human world? No fucking way in hell.

Unless Orson's mother hated her own kind as much as their enemies did, I could never see her willingly hooking up with a dragon. But the alternative didn't make much sense either.

Round and round my thoughts went, trying to make sense of Orson's personal history. Trying to reconcile a member of the territory's ruling pack as being blood-related to an enemy.

He had revealed so little about himself in the time we'd spent together, and yet I got the sense that he had shared more with me than anyone else in his life, including his packmates.

The only thing he'd revealed about his father was that he was a piece of shit.

I sighed and dropped my chin into my hands, taking a break from staring at my dead phone. Really, how could I fault him for not revealing his dragon nature? For keeping it to himself all this time. Fucking moon, it was no wonder he felt friction between himself and well, everyone. How lonely it must have felt to be possibly the only hybrid shifter in existence.

Sick of stewing around in my thoughts, I stood from the crate I'd been sitting on and headed down one of the bunker's many tunnels.

Bare lightbulbs were strung along the ceiling, some of their brackets loose or gone completely, which made the lights hang unevenly. It was amazing they still worked, considering they'd been installed in the sixties or so.

Since the territory borders were drawn, we didn't have much use for these underground shelters anymore. The air was stale despite an elaborate duct system that pulled in fresh air from the surface.

And naturally, we weren't vampires. After three days underground, everyone was getting restless and antsy without sunlight.

I passed by an open door in the tunnel and paused to give a nod and a wave hello to the small werewolf pack in the room. I hadn't known the Dark Fang pack before bunkering down here, but we had the room, so they were more than welcome. The family unit consisted of Silvan, the alpha, his two younger brothers, Camus and Talon, Silvan's mate, Ady, and their two pups.

"Going for another walk, Shiloh?" Camus, the youngest of the adult wolves asked lightheartedly.

"Seeing if there's an update," I replied. "Hey, any chance you guys have a way to charge a phone?"

"Sure do." Silvan leaned up from where he'd been reclined on a cot, cradling one of his sleeping pups against his chest. With a free hand, he pulled out a small generator from under the cot.

"You're a lifesaver, thank you."

"No problem." The alpha stood while I plugged in my charging cord and phone, gently rocking his child as he paced the small room. "We're all waiting for word from the outside world, aren't we?"

"Don't I know it." I headed for the exit to resume my march down the tunnel. "I'll let you guys know what I find out. Thanks again!"

I gave smiles and greetings to other families I

passed, human, witch and werewolf alike. We had roughly three-quarters of the territory's witches and humans in our bunker, and maybe a quarter of the werewolves, not including Howling Death. The wolf population usually had their own bunkers under their pack lodges. But for the especially small packs, like Dark Fang, who might've not had those resources yet, we were happy to share.

At the end of the tunnel, I knocked on the steel door to the central room, which was the largest in our maze of underground bunkers. We called it the command, and it served as a meeting room for those in charge of our communities.

"Come in," called a male voice from the other side.

I turned the wheel in the center of the door to unlatch and then open it. Inside the command was Bodhi, the representative of the humans without magic, and Griselda, the owner of our magical supply shop, Manticore's Cauldron, and chosen leader of witches.

The two of them had no formal titles or duties as the leaders of our respective populations. We were all considered subjects of Howling Death.

"Any news?" I asked after closing the door behind me.

Bodhi shook his head. "The orders from Derric are to remain underground." He pointed to a stack of papers in front of him on the long conference table. "Griselda and I were just re-tallying the stores of food and water. We can stay down here for two more weeks before we have to start rationing."

"Two weeks?" I repeated. "Sweet moon, the poor families in here."

"The young werewolves are finding it especially hard," Griselda added sympathetically. "I've already had to provide anxiety potions to a few. It's not natural for their animal natures to live in such cramped spaces."

"There's been no word at all?" I asked in disbelief. "No sighting of the dragon or anything?"

"We're in contact with Howling Death twice a day," Bodhi answered. "All they tell us is to stay hidden."

That didn't make any sense, and I rubbed my now-unmarked arm as I pondered it.

"If the dragon was flying around causing mayhem, wouldn't the air pulled in here smell like smoke?" I looked between the two leaders. "Isn't it suspicious to both of you that they're saying nothing?"

"I trust Derric," Griselda said. "The alpha is not entitled to tell us everything to keep us safe."

"I understand that, but they should tell us something." I held my hand out. "Where's the phone? I'm calling them."

"What?" Bodhi squawked. "You can't!"

"Why not?"

"Well, because I just got off the phone with them an hour ago. And you can't just *call* Howling Death, they're very busy!"

"Watch me. Phone?"

Griselda chuckled as she stood from the table, then handed me a big brick of a satellite phone from a shelf against the concrete wall. "Can't ever stop a witch from what she puts her mind to."

"Thank you," I said before dialing the Howling Death lodge's landline.

After three rings, someone picked up with a gruff, "Yeah, Howling Death."

"Hi. Um, it's Shiloh."

"Shiloh, hey." The voice softened into a friendly tone. "It's Ruse. How you holding up?"

I didn't know Derric's second-in-command well, except that Ruse had always been polite to me and a good tipper at the bar, despite occasionally getting rowdy after a few too many drinks.

"Good, thanks," I answered him. "Just hanging in, you know."

"We're doing everything we can," the werewolf told me earnestly. "I'm manning the phones for another hour or so, then I'm heading out to join the search. No one's giving up."

Something about his tone made me think there was a disconnect between what the two of us were talking about.

"So, you're still searching for the dragon?" I asked. "There's been no sign of him?"

There was a long pause on the other end. "Fucking moon, has no one told you?"

"Told me what?" My voice went shrill, hand cramping as I gripped the heavy phone harder. "What are you talking about?"

Ruse hesitated a long while before speaking again. I was just about to demand an explanation when he said, "We are still searching for the dragon, yes. There's been no sign of him since that day at your place."

That didn't bode well. Did the mark just disappear for no reason, then?

"Okay, what else?"

There was another long pause.

"Damn it, Ruse. If you don't tell me—"

"We haven't seen Orson since that day either."

While I remained in shocked silence, he went on. "Tryn found Orson's truth thread to be intact, so the dragon was lying about him being involved, as we figured. But after that, the whole pack went out searching, and Orson went out on his own. No one's seen either of them, and we haven't found a trail yet."

Even with an intense sense of wrongness in my chest, I was able to find my voice. "Well, where have you looked?"

"Everywhere in the main parts of the territory and the foothills. We haven't gone up the mountains yet, but are planning on it. It just takes more coordination since we'll be out there for days, if not weeks." Ruse sighed. "Shiloh, I don't want to say we're expecting the worst, but..."

"But you are," I supplied.

"I'm really sorry, Shiloh. We won't stop until we find *something*, but no expectations on what that will be."

"You expect to find a...a body." I forced out the final word. "Or whatever the dragon left of him."

"If the dragon killed him, I feel like we would've seen the dragon by now. So I really don't know."

It took effort but I was finally able to loosen my grip on the phone. "You think there's a chance he's still alive?"

"I hope so. We aren't super close but it would be devastating to lose a packmate." Ruse paused. "I don't recall if you two were officially mated, but I can't imagine how hard this is for you too."

"We weren't—er, aren't yet, but thank you for saying that."

Silence stretched over the phone until Ruse said, "I'm on the next search team, so I should get going. If we find anything, you'll be my first call."

"Thank you, Ruse," I said. "I'll wait to hear from you."

I hung up the phone and immediately left the command center, heading back down the tunnel. With a quick stop to retrieve my barely-charged phone, I returned to the air mattress that had been my home for the last three days. I bundled up in a few layers of clothes, packed some nonperishable food in a bag, then threw a large coat on over everything. Once all bundled and packed up, I headed down a side tunnel, the one that ended in a metal staircase welded into the wall and the hatch leading outside at the top of the staircase.

Nobody was around or guarding anything. We weren't prisoners down here. Everyone just assumed staying down here was common sense—better to do as the wolves said and stay underground while there was a dragon flying around our territory.

But I wasn't operating on common sense anymore. And I would not be sitting around waiting for Ruse to call.

Pushing open the round, metal hatch, I sucked in a greedy breath of the fresh, cool air. Oh, how I missed the outside. Having air pulled underground held nothing on getting it straight from the source.

After pulling myself up to the surface, I closed the latch as quietly as I could. It wouldn't take long for folks to notice me missing, but hopefully no one would be foolish enough to follow.

It was night out, and I stood to my full height and gazed up at the moon. She was a sliver now, growing thinner until she would be reborn as a new moon, and then her magic would ramp up again for the next cycle.

I closed my eyes in deference to her, to her magic that nourished this land and the people in it. To her will and the mate she chose for me.

The mate I *would* find, with the magic of our bond to guide me. Orson hadn't bitten me to seal the bond in place, nor had I taken from his flesh, but the thread of our fate was still there, linking us.

I just had to call upon the magic, to find it. And then use it to find him. With the moon waning in power, it wouldn't be as easy. But this was my only option. I had to make it work.

"Please, mother moon," I whispered, tilting my head back with my arms limp at my sides in offering. "Please let me find him."

The darkness behind my closed eyelids brightened into a dark silvery color, and a question was posed. Not with words exactly, but I immediately knew I had to answer for something.

"I accept him for who he is," I told the night air. "It doesn't matter his origins, his blood relations to the dragons. No matter what, Orson is a son of yours. Your magic runs in him, and he is a strong, capable werewolf. Fate has chosen him for me, and I accept him with all that I am. I..." My breath hitched as a sob threatened to choke my words, but I swallowed. "I was wrong to reject him. So very wrong. I...love him."

A cool breeze picked up and caressed my cheek. When I opened my eyes, all the joy and hope I hadn't dared to feel before now soared in my chest.

I saw a silver thread, delicate and ethereal as spider's silk, stretching from the crown of my head into the mountains.

"Thank you, sweet moon," I whispered in awe before hurrying to follow the path laid out for me.

The path that would lead me to my mate.

CHAPTER 24

ORSON

Something was touching me. Why I was even alive enough to perceive touch, I had no idea.

My sense of smell was dulled. Either that or my nose was broken beyond repair, because I could not smell anything around me. I opened my eyes, slowly and painstakingly, and could make out shapes and colors. So was I human then?

"You took quite a beating, big brother."

I startled at the female voice and instantly regretted it. The small movement sent pain shooting up my neck into my head.

"Hold still," the voice chastised. She was so familiar to me and yet utterly foreign. There was a slight accent that took me too long to place.

It was the same accent I had before I was brought into Howling Death.

"Nova," I gasped in disbelief. "What are you doing here?"

"Healing you." The pressure of her hand moved to a

different area of my torso. "I could smell your blood and hear your howls from miles away."

I blinked and the world around me started to sharpen, details filtering in. I saw the tops of trees and the sky above them. Turning my head, I saw a small clearing and a forest floor that looked like a battle had taken place. Once I could focus up close, I saw her tending to me. My half-sister.

Nova was dressed in an outfit of rough elk hide, a fur-lined hood covering her head and the top half of her face. Her hands hovered over my left thigh, her lips tight in concentration as an open, frost-bitten wound returned to normal color and mended itself back together.

"What happened?" I demanded. "If you're here, where's the pack?"

"In their normal territory," she said distractedly. "I've been spending time on my own lately."

"Why?"

She shrugged, the movement barely perceptible under all the thick hides she wore. "Lately, I prefer being alone over being treated like an outsider."

"So you still can't shift," I surmised. "Ever think about how dangerous it is to be alone out here when you're barely more than a human?"

"Leave it to you to lecture me when you're on death's doorstep." Nova dropped her hands and pushed back her hood, revealing her narrowed dark eyes and red, wind-chapped cheeks. "Funny how you're part wolf, dragon, *and* human, and you're still in worse shape than me."

I shot straight up and immediately hissed at the sharp pain running up from my hip. "Ah, fuck. The dragon! Where is he? What happened? The last thing I remember, I..." I trailed off, too stunned to voice the memory. How cold I had felt on the inside, the urge to vomit. Only instead of my food, I had blasted Mokir with a stream of pure ice.

From my fucking mouth.

Like...an ice dragon? He'd said something about them, hadn't he?

"You're leaning on him." Nova nodded at my shoulder.

I looked behind me and recoiled as much as was physically possible in my current state. "Fucking hell!" The school bus-sized animal was lying completely still, no breath or animation to be seen.

"He was dead when I got here," my sister said. "Looked like he'd collapsed on top of you, so I pulled you out, but your leg looked fucked, so I didn't want to drag you too far." She gave me a strange look. "Looks like he's got bad frostbite around some belly and chest wounds. I'd bet you his heart is frozen solid."

"Well that's a metaphor I'm too tired to interpret right now."

She returned to prodding around my injuries. "I took care of the worst damage I could, but I'm tapped out. Your hip or pelvis is probably broken. Normally I'd suggest shifting, but that could be even worse for your bones and tissue."

I watched her stand up and dust off her hands. "So, that's it? You're just leaving?"

"I've done all I can for you, big brother. You know how taxing the healing is on me. I have to recover."

"You could come with me," I suggested, and not for the first time. "Stay in Vargmore proper. Join Howling Death. They'd love to have a healer like you."

She shook her head. "No. Living in a town with all that technology you talk about? It's not for me."

"It can't be any worse than a feral pack that ostracizes you to the point of being in the wilderness alone."

"It'll be exactly the same." Nova crossed her arms, tucking her hands inside her sleeves. "A pack who will never accept me because I cannot shift. Or your human population who will find me too wild. At least here I can be on my own terms."

"You're vulnerable out here. Unprotected."

She cocked her head, eying the dead dragon on the ground behind me. "I can handle myself."

"I know you can," I sighed. "If there ever comes a time where you don't want to live like this anymore, just remember you don't have to be alone."

Nova lifted her hood and resettled it on her head. "It was good to see you, Orson. Best return to your pack. And your mate."

She turned and started off through the woods without another word, without a chance for me to ask how the hell she knew I had a mate. Or to refute the statement, since Shiloh decided she was no longer mine.

Although for all I knew, Nova had known since she was born. Like Tryn, she had a way of knowing certain things. She once told me she believed it was the moon's way of making up for not giving her a wolf that could live outside of her skin.

She hid it well, but I knew she yearned deeply for the ability to shift. That ability defined us as werewolves, and I hated that she felt so fundamentally different and cut off from the rest of us. We bonded over our differences to other wolves, and even if we weren't close, I wanted to remain a presence in her life.

If I could get off this mountain alive, that was.

I looked at my surroundings, trying to get a sense of

something that wasn't this pain that continued to shoot up my body. The sun was setting and it would be dusk soon. If I really couldn't shift, I had to get out of here before I froze to death in my naked human skin.

Taking my hands behind me, I pressed against the dragon's flank, using the support to come to my feet. My left side was pulsing with heat and pain, like Mokir's ghost was still roasting me with his breath. I kept my weight on my right side as I hobbled up toward the dragon's head, using his neck spikes like handholds.

I needed a walking stick, something to help hold me up as I made my way down the mountain. Back to my pack. To my mate.

While searching the ground, I wondered how Shiloh would react to learning I'd killed the dragon that terrorized her. She would be relieved, I hoped. She would sleep peacefully at night knowing she was safe.

And as much as I hoped she realized that I had no loyalty to Mokir, that he meant nothing to me and being my brother didn't change the fact that I wanted to kill him the moment I knew someone was threatening her, I knew chances were slim that she would welcome me back as her mate.

"It's something I'm prepared to live with," I said to the open-mouthed dragon's head lying on the ground. "No thanks to you. But as long as you're not around to touch my mate, it's fucking worth it."

Anger welled up inside me. In a sense, this dragon had brought Shiloh and I together. It was the smell of her fear that sent my protective instincts into overdrive. But he'd also ruined us. He would get no credit for leading me to the love of my life, no space in my head.

But maybe I would take something of him. To always remember what I'd done for her.

Shakily I went down into a crouch, my left hip screaming as I reached into that mouth with so many teeth. I wrapped my hand around one long fang and gave it a hard yank.

The tooth broke off after a few tries, and then I had it, a little trophy of my victory. Looking at it would always be bittersweet, but I accomplished the most important thing; keeping my mate safe.

Once I had the dragon's tooth, I tested out a few branches on the ground before finding a suitable walking stick, then it was time to get moving.

Fuck me, it was already getting dark. Leaning heavily on my makeshift cane, I went out into the clearing to see what might be left of my clothes. Most of it was burnt tatters, but I pulled on what was left of my pants and shirt, then wrapped the dragon tooth in another scrap of fabric.

Only the setting sun could tell me which way led back toward town, and I started at a glacial pace in that direction. I was alive, but everything hurt and the temperature was dropping fast. Plus, it would be pitch-black soon. I needed my wolf senses and his fur to keep me warm.

I called to my animal within me, but he refused to budge. He already didn't like the pain we were in and was concerned about a shift making it worse, like Nova had said. Normally shifters healed quickly, and while I was glad to not be on death's door anymore, my weakened state was still nothing to write home about. I needed to get out of the wilderness if I wanted to survive, and I needed to reach civilization fast.

Darkness came swiftly, and the waning moon's light did not offer me much guidance. I pulled forth as much as my wolf senses as I could without shifting and still felt totally lost in the dark. And it was really fucking cold again, even with no ice-fire building inside me this time. Just the heat of my normal breaths and my chattering teeth.

The cold just made all my aches and pains worse. My left side was screaming, my head pounded, and I could no longer feel my fingers and toes. It was starting to dawn on me that my sister's healing was all for naught. I could still very well die out here.

The pain, the cold, all of it, made it impossible to tune into my senses and keep track of where I was going. I tripped over something, a rock, a root, I didn't fucking know because my feet were numb, and went tumbling.

I curled up and tried to roll down the terrain, but it felt like getting stabbed over and over on my bad side. Something hard finally stopped me, a boulder or a tree, who the hell knew? Running my frozen fingers over myself, I felt a warm, sticky wetness on my forehead. Great, so I was bleeding again. *Sorry, sis. All that effort for nothing.*

I relaxed into my position, utterly exhausted and numb. This was it for me. It was a shit deal and honestly embarrassing that I would've succumbed to the elements instead of fighting with a dragon. But I truly could not go on any longer. All my strength was being wasted on shivering and my chattering teeth.

The pack would find me eventually, and the dragon tooth would give them an idea of what happened. Who knew if they'd find the scaly bastard himself, hardly any wolves went that high up the mountain. Someone would, one day. Maybe alien paleontologists millions of years from now would find his fossilized remains.

It didn't matter. Nothing mattered except that Shiloh was safe.

Just as I was about to succumb to the darkness, a single point of light zipped across my vision. It could have been a comet, or a lightning bug, except that I wasn't looking at the sky, and it was too damn cold up here for lightning bugs.

The light swung back toward the direction it came from. And through the painful numbness in my ears, I thought I heard a voice calling out my name.

It had to the moon, her magic taking on a human voice to usher me into the afterlife. That had to be it. The light must have been from her too, but why did it keep swinging back and forth?

"Orson, is that you? Oh my God, Orson!"

The voice sounded frantic, panicked, and so familiar. I couldn't decide if it was sweet or cruel for the moon to take on the voice of the mate I had lost.

"Orson! I'm right here, stay with me." Hands touched my face that were so warm, the heat was almost searing. "Fucking moon, you're a block of ice. Hang on, I'm going to get you warmed up."

The scent of citrus and cinnamon hit me with a blast of warmth and aching familiarity. Shiloh was...here?

"Shi..." My weak attempt to say her name was thwarted by warm fingers on my dry, freezing lips.

"Don't say a word. I'm getting you to town and then we'll talk." My mate's voice was strong and self-assured, despite the undercurrent of fear I smelled on her.

I wanted to tell her there was no reason to be afraid. The dragon was dead. She, the pack, and the entire territory was safe.

But I succumbed to exhaustion before that could happen.

CHAPTER 25
SHILOH

I never thought I'd be one of those witches who took up embroidery. But stabbing a needle through something over and over was the only activity that gave me some sense of calm while waiting for my mate to recover from his injuries.

Orson was in remarkable shape for what he'd been through, according to the team of healer witches who tended to him. Aside from having a shockingly low internal body temperature for a werewolf, he only had minor surface injuries and a fractured pelvis.

On my way down the mountain with him, I had called Howling Death and shouted over the alpha to have a team of healers ready at the edge of town. Derric got over being pissed at me quickly enough to do as I asked, even calling an angel friend in case we needed more powerful healing magic.

Thankfully, all the extra healers were overkill, and the main priority was bringing Orson's temperature back up. The next forty-eight hours were a blur of gradually warming him with blankets and warm fluids. He came in and out of consciousness the whole time and didn't seem to be fully present when he was awake, which worried me. But waiting was all I could do.

A few of the healers noted that it was unusual for his temperature to be so low. It was cold in the mountains at night but not dangerous-levels-of-hypothermia cold. A lot of people had questions that only Orson had the answers to, so it was a waiting game for everyone.

His computers hummed quietly, making a gentle white noise in his room at the Howling Death lodge. The only other sounds were his breaths and my threaded needle stabbing through the fabric stretched over my embroidery hoop. His temperature had finally stabilized late last night. His vitals were strong and his other injuries were well on their way to repairing themselves, thanks to his shifter healing.

All I needed was for my mate to open those brilliant, arctic eyes and see me, recognize me. Tell me if he would still let me be his mate after what I did.

It was past noon when I set aside my embroidery hoop and stretched out my cramped hand. I twisted in my chair and stretched out my hunched back as I stood. I'd find something in the lodge kitchen to nibble on and come right back. It wasn't like I had much of an appetite, but sustenance would keep me going.

With a final lingering glance at my mate, I headed for the door and—

"Shiloh?"

I froze in place, then whipped around. Orson's head rolled slowly on the pillow to face me, then his eyes started peeling open. "That really you, sweet witch?" he asked in a hoarse voice.

I must have levitated across the floor because I could

not recall how I went from the door to the spot in bed beside him.

"Orson! How do you feel? What do you need? Are you cold? Too hot?" I touched his forehead, his neck, and slightly flushed cheeks. It was such a relief to see color and life back in him.

"No, I'm okay." He coughed as he started to sit up. "Little thirsty, maybe."

"Here, don't move. I got it." I reached for the bedside table and handed him a mug of tea, which was infused with cinnamon, echinacea, chamomile, orange peel, and a touch of amplifying magic so the herbs would give an extra boost to his immune system.

He downed the whole thing in a few gulps before setting it aside. Before I could ask anything else, he blurted out, "My mother was a feral wolf who didn't know about our conflict with the vampires or that the dragons sided with them. She was isolated from all that."

My mouth opened. Shut. Then opened again as I said, "Okay."

"She ran into my father, a dragon shifter, during her pack's regular nomadic traveling before the borders were established. Her pack often went to the desert regions during the cold seasons. She mated with my father and decided to leave the pack to be with him."

"Orson, you don't have to—"

"Yes I do," he insisted, eyes sharp on my face, his jaw set tight. "Please just let me get this out, Shiloh."

At my hesitant nod, he kept going.

"The minute he got her isolated from her pack, he became abusive toward her. She also didn't know that he had another mate, a dragon like him, and already had a son with her."

As Orson told me his mother's story, the words came out of him in sharp, angry punches. It was almost like he'd been dying to tell this to someone for years but the habit of keeping his secret hidden created resistance for him.

"My mother felt trapped, especially after finding out she was pregnant with me. When she had me, she pretty much raised me on her own. My father spent most of his time with his real family. When he did come by, he brought Mokir along to play with me, so he said. But he only ever came over to fight with my mother, and my half-brother took the opportunity to abuse me."

"Orson," I breathed, reaching for his hand on top of the blanket. "I'm so sorry."

He didn't seem to notice the touch but carried on with his story. "When my shifter traits started presenting, I only showed wolf features. My dad warned my mother that if my animal wasn't a dragon, I was worthless and we'd be kicked out of 'his' territory." Orson let out a light scoff at the memory. "I had my first full shift a few years later, and sure enough, I was all wolf. Not a scale or dragon wing on me."

"So he made you leave?" I squeezed his hand and got a light squeeze in return.

"Yeah. Flew us over and dropped us in the middle of the wilderness. I was still pretty bouncy then, but Mom broke her leg from that fall."

"Fuck, that's so cruel."

"We found one of the feral packs, but by then, word had reached them that the dragons aligned themselves with our enemies and that my mom had gone off with one of them. So, we weren't exactly welcomed with open arms."

"That's terrible. She didn't know, she was a victim."

"One male took pity on her or something, I dunno."

Orson sighed, looking exhausted. "They weren't in love or anything, but they mated with an arrangement in place. She would get his protection, he would get a pup of his own. Only that didn't work out, because that pup was born defective."

"Your sister that can't shift?"

"Yeah. She was the one that found me out there, stitched me up to the best of her ability after I thought that dragon had ended me."

"You thought?" I repeated. "So the dragon is...?"

"Dead," he confirmed with a solemn nod. "You'll never have to see his scaly face again."

I brought an arm forward, showing that the mark had disappeared. "I knew it."

The first twitches of a smile played on Orson's lips, but his overall expression remained remote. "No trace of him left. I'm glad."

I scooted closer, releasing his hand to run a caress up his arm. "It's such a relief he's gone, but I hate that we nearly lost you. Why didn't you say anything to the pack?"

"Because it's *my* duty to protect my mate."

My heart went wild at the conviction in his voice, how quickly he'd given that answer, like it was the simplest, most obvious one in the world. "Orson—"

"Wait, don't say anything yet. I have more to tell you."

"Okay." I settled back against his pillows, keeping my hand on his arm. I never wanted to stop touching him.

"I came to Howling Death about ten years ago, after running into Tryn," he went on, focusing on a random spot on the blanket. "He saw how clearly I didn't get along with the feral pack and said I would belong here. It's been a struggle for me, learning the ways of a pack that's *not* feral, but I did feel like I belonged here more than anywhere else."

"Did?" The past tense use of the word scared me.

Orson pulled in a deep breath and lowered his voice. "I think I might have a little dragon in me after all."

I stared at him. "How?"

"Remember what Mokir said about my eyes? That I have the eyes of our ice dragon ancestors? Well, I was able to kill him because..." Orson didn't speak for a long time. "Because I breathed ice. Ice-fire. Something like that. I was so out of it, but I'm pretty sure that's what killed him. I froze his internal organs."

Orson leaned back against his headboard and looked at me, his expression apprehensive. "Do you believe me?"

"Yes, I do." I squeezed his arm. "That probably explains your hypothermia. Your insides had to be freezing for that to occur."

"Sure as hell felt like they were." His expression hardened, his emotions closing off. "You know everything about me now, more than anyone else. I'm sorry I wasn't honest with you before. Not just about me but the cameras too. Everything that I've fucked up."

"It's okay. You had your reasons." I was so close to him, I was practically in his lap. But his closed-off body language and his hard expression kept me on edge. "I'm sorry I accused you of working with Mokir. I...I can't believe I jumped to that conclusion."

"Your trust in me was already shaken. I don't blame you for that."

"Well, you should, because it was a pretty big accusation. You deserve better than that."

"And you deserve a mate who doesn't hide things from you."

I reached up to stroke the dark shadow of beard on his

cheek, trying to catch the gaze of those incredible eyes. "Well, nothing is hidden anymore, right?"

Finally he looked directly at me, a sliver of vulnerability peeking through his emotionless mask. "No, and it never will be. I'll always be an open book to you."

"And you did slay a dragon for me, so." I allowed a smile to pull at my lips. "How many can say their mates did that?"

Orson pulled in a sharp breath, his mask crumbling. "You still want to be my mate?" he whispered.

"I *am* your mate. I never stopped being that." I brought a hand to the nape of his neck and rested my forehead against his temple. "And I accept you wholly and completely as you are. Dragon, wolf, human, all of the above; I don't care. You are mine, Orson, and I've already made this vow to the moon. It was she who led me to you."

Finally, the last of his defenses melted away. Orson turned his head, his forehead rolling against mine. "You mean that?" he asked in a rough whisper, like he couldn't believe it.

"With every bone in my body." My fingers scraped through his hair. "I'm sorry I ever made you doubt. I never will again." I lifted my face away just enough to look at him clearly. "Will you still have me as yours?" A stab of fear hit me at the idea that he might not trust *me* anymore.

Orson wrapped a large palm around my nape, bringing his forehead to mine again and our noses to touch. His breath fanned over my lips as he spoke.

"With my whole heart and the moon magic in each of my cells. With every strand of DNA that makes me man and wolf, you, Shiloh, are the mate for me. *All* of me."

The kiss he initiated started out as soft and tender. I opened my mouth with a gasp, an invitation for his tongue to lick inside. And then it became a desperate press and pull on both our ends, the craving for each other maddening, and a rush of emotions.

It was release and relief. The weight of everything felt like it lifted all at once and gave me the sensation of floating. I also started crying because what else would be a better release of everything I was feeling?

"Hey, what?" Orson pulled away with a worried expression, his thumbs dragging over my tears. "What's wrong, my pretty witch?"

I laughed with a sniffle. "Nothing, I promise. I just can't believe it's all over."

"Your nightmare is over." He pressed a kiss to my forehead. "But we're just beginning."

"You're so right." My arms went around his neck while his wrapped around my back. He started pulling me across his lap, which got me scared for another reason. "Orson, wait. You have a pelvic fracture!"

"No idea what that is." He kept hauling me over him and looked adorably annoyed as I hovered over blanket-covered legs.

"You're still healing and shouldn't put any weight on here." I pointed straight down.

My werewolf made a dismissive sound, grabbed my waist and pulled me down right on top of him. I tried to fight the movement but was no match for his strength. All I got was lost balance and careened forward into his chest. His arms went around me again, trapping me in place against his torso and the other hard place just under the covers.

"I feel just fine," he said in a low rumble against my ear. With a sensual lick, he added, "I miss my mate. And this time, I need to mark her."

CHAPTER 26
SHILOH

A thrilling shiver rolled down my spine at Orson's words. Every instinct within me shouted, *Yes! Mark me, claim me.* I felt no doubt or hesitation that he was for me. I wanted to wear his claiming bite proudly and mark him as mine in return.

My only hesitation was when it came to his well being.

"Are you sure you're feeling up to it?" I gave a slight nip to his earlobe. "Maybe you should rest for another day or so."

"I've rested long enough, and I've never been more sure of anything in my life." His hands smoothed down from my waist to cup my ass. "I need to claim you as mine more than I need to breathe."

Well, if that didn't make me swoon. "I just don't want to worsen your injury."

"Seriously, I feel great. Call the healers in to check me over if you want, but they're going to get eyeful of what's happening under this sheet."

Oh hell no. Not a soul outside of this room was going to

see my man naked. I made a growling sound deep in my throat, even though it wasn't a natural impulse.

The sound had the intended effect though, and Orson laughed with a pleased rumble. "You're sexy when you're possessive, my sweet witch."

"I'll make you a deal." Looping my arms around his neck, I leaned back and made a slight roll of my hips over his length.

"Mm, I love making deals with you." His teeth sank into his lip, eyes lighting up.

"We'll do this now—"

"I like where this is going so far."

"—as long as you don't react with any pain or discomfort. The instant I see a wince or a grimace from you, we're stopping and I'm getting a healer in here. And do not take this as a challenge to mask your pain, Orson. I seriously don't want to hurt you."

His wolfish grin faded away as he brought one of my hands to his lips and placed a kiss on my knuckles. "You have my word, Shiloh. If I feel even a twinge of pain, we can stop." He turned my hand and kissed my palm, his lips lingering before speaking again. "And I'm kind of stunned that you care about me so much."

The words hit me with a deep ache, and I brought that palm to Orson's cheek. "Of course I care about you. You're my mate, and it's my job to look out for you." My thumb traced his mouth, my gaze fixated on those lips. "Because I love you, Orson."

He inhaled so sharply, I at first thought it was a hiss of pain. Then his mouth formed a smile warm enough to melt polar ice caps. "I think I've loved you since you first came out of that back room, swinging a bat at me."

"Okay, let's get one thing straight." My smile pressed to his. "I never actually *swung* the bat at you."

"You held it very menacingly."

"Were you afraid for your life?"

"Terrified."

The next thing I knew, the room spun and I was flat on my back with Orson's grinning face hovering above mine.

"See?" He pulled away the blanket that had been pinned between us from the movement. "Right as rain."

I looked down and...yeah, *right* was an appropriate word. He'd been naked under the sheets and looked perfectly well from the waist down. Not to mention happy to see me.

I wrapped my hand around the base of his cock and squeezed my grip as I stroked upward. The resulting moan was toe-curling music to my ears.

"What's that?" I nipped his earlobe again, spreading a bead of precum around his head with my thumb. "Are you in pain, my love?"

"No, don't...don't even play like that." Orson laughed roughly. "You feel so good, I never want you to stop."

"Stop what, this?" I stroked him from head to base and back up again. By my next downward pass, he was thrusting through my fist.

"Yes, that," he groaned before catching my wrist, halting my movement. "But I need you to stop so I can last while I'm inside you."

"Ruining my fun already?" I teased with a fake pout.

He answered by leaning in and biting my stuck-out lip. At the same time, he yanked off my pants in one smooth motion. My shirt and bra came off in a flurry of fabric and rough kisses.

When we were finally skin-to-skin, the weight and

warmth of him was so sweet, I had to sigh out in pleasure. Orson ran his nose down my neck, kissing the hollow of my throat when he got there.

"Where do you want my bite?" He ran kisses from the corner of my jaw to the crook of my neck, then to my shoulder, like he was testing each spot.

"Here." I turned my head, exposing the side of my neck, and pointed right to the center.

Orson purred as his warm fingers caressed over the spot. "Everyone will see."

"Good. That's what I want."

He blinked like he couldn't believe it, and then a crease formed between his eyebrows.

"What is it?" I stroked his cheek, bringing his attention back to my face.

He swallowed and then sighed. "I don't want to hurt you either."

Sweet moon, I didn't know my heart could fit any more love for this wolf.

"I know you would never hurt me. Any pain will be temporary." I held his face in my hands as I kissed him. "I want this, and I want you more than anything."

Not another word needed to be said. Orson met my eyes and lowered another kiss to my mouth. This one was deeper, hungrier, sealing a promise that we both understood without the need to speak.

My legs slid apart so Orson could ease between them. His cock dragged a hot, pulsing touch down my lower belly as he drew his hips back. I gasped into his kiss when his head rested over my clit, the weight of it pressing and teasing my most sensitive spot.

Orson grinned against my lips as he continued to draw back slowly, letting that blunt head drag along my sensitive lips. My pulse pounded between my legs, and every muscle was taut with anticipation.

When he finally pressed forward, my body took him inside with one fluid stroke. The way he stretched and filled me made me arch with a gasp against his mouth.

My arms and legs went around him, gripping his waist with my thighs and scoring my nails down his back. Orson could only retreat from my body so much before sliding deeply back inside where he belonged. Each press forward and drag backward was intentional. Not slow, but I felt every inch with each motion, the friction exquisite and inescapable.

Like me, Orson was savoring every sensation. His mouth roamed over my body just as much as my hands did him, kissing my mouth, my collarbones, my sternum, and teasing the sensitive points of my nipples with his teeth. He always returned to the spot I'd pointed to on my neck, kissing and licking there reverently, as if to prime it for what was to come.

With all the touching and the delicious way he fucked me, my orgasm approached at a slow, steady build. My hips curled up underneath him, angling my clit to take more of the impact, and the pleasure coiled up even faster from there.

"I'm close..." I panted into Orson's ear. "So close...fuck, it's so good..."

A pleased, purring growl vibrated his chest, and he ran his teeth along the pulse in my neck. "That's my sweet witch. Take all you need from me."

I held onto the back of his arms, digging into the flexed muscles as he kept a steady pace, his body crashing into mine in a way that was powerful but unhurried. Looking down between us, it was so hot to watch him move. Even now, he had the fluid grace of an animal despite his bulk and musculature. His abs flexed with every breath, every thrust. His hipbones made a V-shape that pointed right to where he fucked me. Eventually it was the visual that took me over the edge, watching my werewolf mate take me there like my own personal porn film.

The first strike of the orgasm hit my system, and then Orson struck my neck.

It didn't hurt, but heat rushed my body from head to toe like someone swinging a torch over me. Sensations filled me, and I couldn't tell the difference between the mating bond and the orgasm. I felt weightless and clung to Orson's arms so I wouldn't float away into space.

My pulse throbbed between my legs, and I felt something new under my skin, a presence that wasn't there before and definitely wasn't me. In my mind's eye, I saw a beautiful silver wolf with pale blue eyes, and he was happy beyond expression. I knew because I felt it from him, the overjoyed paw taps, the happy spins, and the tail wagging that wouldn't quit.

Hello, Orson's wolf, I greeted him in that mind space.

The wolf gently mouthed on me, his teeth touching down without any pressure behind them. *Mark me too?* he asked, almost bashfully.

Yes, of course. I didn't have a mating bite like a wolf, but right then, I knew instinctively what to do.

Magic concentrated in my fingertips as I returned my awareness to my physical body. Orson was still inside me, his mouth gently licking my neck to soothe his bite. He must have noticed the instant I came back online because he pulled away to stare at my face. "Are you okay?"

I kissed him in reply, squeezing around his cock internally to encourage him to resume. "Your wolf is such a good boy," I sighed dreamily.

He moaned at that, the sound something between relief and pleasure. His cock was rigid as stone as he moved through me, his pace becoming frenzied as he panted harder. Like he had done, I wanted his orgasm at the same moment I marked him.

Under my skin, I could feel his emotions if I concentrated. His relief that he didn't hurt me, his love and reverence for my body, for me. I felt the tension in his muscles, the pounding of his heart as he fought to hold his orgasm back.

Oh, that was going to be fun to mess with later.

But right now, I wanted to give him exactly what he gave to me.

"Is here good?" My fingertips, charged with magic, trailed from his shoulder down his arm.

"Anywhere," he growled. "I don't care, just make me yours."

I wrapped my other arm around his back and brought my mouth to his ear. "Then come for me, my love."

His pleasure surged through the bond, but he still did not release. A dry chuckle left his mouth. "After you."

The pressure of his fingers slid over my clit, and my laugh quickly morphed into a moan as he coaxed another orgasm out of me. This time, we came together.

Along with my physical release, magic pulsed through my fingertips as my nails dug into his skin. On the next pulse, I dragged them down, scratching deeply into Orson's arm. I felt the flash of pain from his end, but it was quickly followed by the overwhelming tidal wave of pleasure as he spilled inside me.

It was the strangest, most beautiful thing I ever felt, my partner's orgasm alongside my own.

The storm of sensations calmed and it was just us, my mate and I together. I stroked Orson's arm where I'd scratched him and leaned up to inspect them closer. Four vertical lines ran through his skin, tinged with red that was quickly fading, thanks to shifter healing. The fifth mark, made by my thumb, hung slightly apart from the others.

"They don't hurt." Orson kissed my temple. "I can feel you worrying over me, and you don't have to."

"So it worked." I traced the lines in fascination. I hadn't known what to do, how to mark my werewolf mate, until the very moment it needed to happen.

"That's us." He pressed a kiss to the tender skin on my neck where he'd marked me. "You and I, we make it work."

My chest swelled with my own joy alongside his. "We do, don't we?"

"We do." He kissed my eyelids. "And until our souls return home to the moon, we will," he vowed.

EPILOGUE
ORSON

"Stop. They're not worth the effort," I said.

Shiloh looked aghast, slapping a dish towel over her shoulder. "I still can't believe the things that come out of your mouth sometimes."

I shrugged, resting one bare ass cheek on the barstool across from her. "It's the truth."

"They're your pack." She raised a glass to the light to inspect it. "Well, I guess they're my pack too, aren't they?"

"Yes." Warmth flooded my chest, a mix of hers and mine, from the bond. "Because you're mine, you're part of Howling Death now too."

She turned her head, smiling as she placed the glass on the bar. "Do I get an initiation ritual like Riley?"

"If you want." I shrugged. "You'll be a hell of a slow poke on two legs during the runs though."

Shiloh snorted in reply. The pale scars of my mating bite on her slender neck caught the overhead light, making my cock thicken. I wanted to kiss that tender spot, taste her fluttering pulse under my lips as I felt that same rhythm inside her.

But it seemed my mate had other plans. Like being hospitable.

I'd found my mate in full-on work mode, sweeping the floor, wiping down tables, warming up the pizza oven, and putting on a fresh keg of beer. The rest of the pack was heading this way, to Stout & Spirit, once finished with the full moon run. I'd run ahead, having a stash of clothes at Shiloh's apartment, although I was currently naked and had hoped to not wear anything for what I had in mind.

It was just the two of us for now, and I wanted to make every second count.

"So *my* pack is going to be hungry and thirsty after this run, right?" Shiloh held her palms out. "So why wouldn't I be a good host?"

"Because they're still more wolves than human, on top of being rowdy and moon drunk. Like, hopefully none of them piss on your chair legs."

"They would never!"

"Get over here," I growled, tired of arguing with her.

The mating bond flared with Shiloh's amusement and her stubbornness. "If you want me so bad, come and get me."

There was a momentary standoff, and then I hauled myself over the bar, swiping an arm out for my mate.

I barely missed, and with a shriek, Shiloh took off running toward the back door. I chased after her and caught up in three strides, wrapping my arms around her waist and lifting her off the ground to her shrieking laughter.

"Oh, where to sink into you before we have an audience?" I nibbled her neck as I turned in a circle. "Hm, on top of the dishwasher? Or the counter? Maybe I could just bend you over these kegs."

Just as I was about to come to a decision, the roar of motorcycles floated up the road into Stout & Spirit's driveway.

"Fuck." I rested my forehead on the back of Shiloh's head while she patted my arm sympathetically.

"Go get dressed, and I promise we'll get good and naked once everyone leaves again."

"Tell them you're closed," I groaned into her neck.

"I tried that on you and it didn't work, remember?"

I laughed, setting her gently on her feet. "But we do work."

"We do," she agreed, kissing my shoulder where her marks were displayed.

"Tell them I'll be right down."

With a final kiss, I released her and went out the rear door to the stairs leading up to her apartment. I let myself in, then hastily dressed in one of the few changes of clothes I kept here.

Since officially mating two weeks ago, Shiloh and I spent days at a time at each other's places. We talked briefly about getting our own place but were in no rush. We just wanted to enjoy being newly mated, it didn't matter where we laid our heads at night as long as we were together.

Even though it was well into autumn and the nights were getting cooler, I pulled on a sleeveless T-shirt. Ever since Shiloh had left her marks in my arm, I wanted to show them off. Likewise, she'd taken to wearing tops that showed off her neck and wore her hair up more often.

And through our bond, we could feel how much the other loved showing their claim.

In the drawer I kept my clothes, I reached toward the back, hunting for the small box I'd stashed there last week.

With a quick peek under the lid, I knew tonight was the night to give it to her.

The full moon was out, and we had the whole pack under one roof. What better time than now? I stuck the box in my jeans pocket and headed out.

The bar was already lively with noise as I came down the stairs, but two figures stood next to the back door, talking quietly away from the party. I inhaled and picked up the scents of Tryn and Fallon.

"Hey guys," I greeted them when I hit the ground. "What are you doing back here?"

Tryn was frowning, his thick brow pinched and his arms crossed in front of him. "I don't get it," he muttered. "I've never seen it before."

"Seen what?" I looked at Fallon for answers, but he remained tight-lipped.

"There's a fate thread extending from me out to the distance." Tryn pointed in the direction he was looking, but there was nothing distinctive in sight besides the moon, sky, and the dark silhouettes of the woods.

"Okay, so?"

The other wolf looked at me sharply. "I've never been able to see my own fate threads before. Ever. This is unprecedented, and it's freaking me out."

"Oh." Yeah, I'd remembered him telling me that before.

"I told him there's a portal to the human world that way," Fallon said, looking at Tryn. "Looks like your destiny takes you to the land of humans, my man."

Tryn just shook his head. "Impossible," he muttered.

They both stared at the horizon as if scrutinizing the stars for answers.

"Well, how about a drink?" I suggested. "Shiloh made the place all nice for the pack."

"That sounds like a great idea." Fallon clapped Tryn on the shoulder. "Come on. Maybe moon magic is just extra potent right now. If you still see your thread after tonight, worry about it then."

Tryn grudgingly accepted, and the three of us headed inside through the back door. The bar was packed full of Howling Death wolves, raucous laughter and howling echoing throughout the building. Shiloh was thankfully not serving anyone but letting them help themselves. My mate was talking to Riley, who was perched on one of the barstools while Sawyer poured.

"Hey there, Mr. Freeze," the enforcer greeted.

Ruse coughed up his beer laughing, but I just groaned and rolled my eyes as I walked past. It was a new nickname every day ever since I told them how I'd killed Mokir. Mr. Freeze was the most common, but there was also Ice Breath, Ice Ice Orson, and Elsa.

"Now that we're all here." Sawyer slid a beer over to me and lifted his own. I had just found my spot at Shiloh's side when the enforcer raised his voice. "Riley and I have an announcement to make."

Alright then, I thought as the pack fell into silence. The box in my back pocket could wait a little longer.

From the face-splitting grins on Riley and Sawyers' faces and the intense love shining in their eyes, I had an idea of what the news would be.

"We're having pups!" Sawyer cried at the top of his lungs.

"Well, one for now," Riley corrected him gently.

"At least one!" he bellowed.

The room exploded into cheers, howls, applause, and toasting drinks. Shiloh wrapped Riley in a hug while

Sawyer was hauled out from behind the bar for rough embraces and back slaps.

The beer kept flowing, and the party continued in celebration of the couple's happy news. Eventually, I was able to pull my tipsy mate into a somewhat quiet corner. "I have a gift for you," I said into her ear before kissing her mark again because I just couldn't help myself.

"Gift? For me?" She stared up at me with dilated eyes.

"Who else?" I chuckled as I held out the box to her.

Shiloh hesitated before accepting it. I took a long pull of my beer to chase away the nerves, and her head immediately snapped up. "Why are you nervous?"

"I just...I dunno. Open it. If you don't like it or it's not appropriate, maybe spare my feelings and don't tell me."

She made a dismissive sound. "How could I not like a gift from you?"

"Because I'm still me."

"And I love you no matter what, remember?"

"I love you too. Now open it before I have a stroke."

With a laugh, she lifted the lid of the shallow box and gasped at what lay on the tissue paper inside. "Orson, is this...?"

"Yes," I confirmed.

She lifted the delicate chain and stared at the polished dragon tooth strung on via a hole drilled through the top. I'd had to sneak away to visit the witch metalsmith in town to make my trophy a proper necklace for my mate.

"My wolf wanted to bring you his entire head," I explained. "But even I know that's a little overkill."

"Just a little," she laughed. "Orson, this is brutal and... perfect. I love it."

The bubbling happiness and pride shining through the bond told me she wasn't lying. She was proud of me for what I'd done. I had proven myself a protective, worthy mate after all.

"I'm glad you like it," I said through a tight throat. "I wasn't sure if you would."

"Are you kidding? I'll never take it off." She was already bringing the ends of the chain to clasp around her nape. "Who else can say their werewolf mate slayed a dragon and have a necklace to prove it?"

The fang hung just below the hollow of her throat. She looked like a warrior wearing it. "Who else can say their mate was brave enough to stand up to a dragon for the safety of the whole territory?" I cupped her face, my thumb tracing her cheek while my fingers brushed her neck.

She smiled, running her hand up my arm to my neck. "I was decently brave, I guess. But you did the slaying."

"And I'm still in awe of you," I whispered. "I still can't believe the moon blessed me with you as my mate."

"Well." Shiloh wound both hands around my neck, pressing herself flush to me. "We've got centuries to get used to it, don't we?"

"Yes," I breathed before pulling my brilliant, beautiful mate into a kiss.

I savored her taste of cinnamon and citrus as if it was the first time those flavors had woken up my senses.

And I knew, for the centuries to come with my sweet witch at my side, tasting her would always feel like the first time.

)))))♦♦◀◀((((

Thank you so much for reading Enemy Wolf! Are you dying to know Sawyer and Riley's story?
Read it now in Traitor Wolf!

》》》🌘🌑🌒《《《

Want to see even more inside Orson's head, especially when he's jealous?
Click here to download a free bonus scene!

ALSO BY SOPHIE ASH

<u>Gods and Myths</u>

The Minotaur

<u>Howling Death MC</u>

Traitor Wolf

Enemy Wolf

About the Author

Sophie Ash is a USA Today bestselling author from Northern California, writing paranormal motorcycle clubs with plenty of bite, as well as passionate retellings of myths and folklore.

When she's not writing, she's probably reading, gardening, vacuuming up cat hair, or enjoying a craft beer in the sun.

crystalashbooks.com

facebook.com/Crystal.Sophie.Ash.Books

instagram.com/crystalsophieash

amazon.com/author/sophieash

bookbub.com/profile/sophie-ash